TH

Curupira—the wild man—was what the primitive natives of the Amazon basin called Luiz Manchete, and Rebel soon realised how he had earned the name when she found herself alone with him in the heart of his jungle kingdom. She found him fascinating—but she soon learned that his only love would ever be the Amazon ...

THE WILD MAN

BY

MARGARET ROME

MILLS & BOON LIMITED
15–16 BROOK'S MEWS
LONDON W1A 1DR

First published 1980
Australian copyright 1980
Philippine copyright 1980
This edition 1980

© Margaret Rome 1980

ISBN 0 263 73387 4

Set in Linotype Times 11 on 12½ pt.

*Made and printed in Great Britain by
Richard Clay (The Chaucer Press) Ltd., Bungay, Suffolk*

CHAPTER ONE

'NOT long now until touchdown, *senhorita*. I estimate that our plane will land within the next fifteen minutes.'

'How can you possibly tell?' Rebel queried, peering for the umpteenth time at terrain that was utterly devoid of landmarks. For what seemed hours the small bush plane had flown over a sea of forest, a monotonous green wilderness stretching unbroken to every limit of the horizon: the Amazon basin, one of the last places on earth only vaguely known to man, containing within its density areas where no white man had ever set foot, where the only roads were rivers, and where there were regions which on Brazilian government maps had the words *regiao inexplorado*, region unexplored, scrawled across their surface. For centuries this area had drawn like a magnet explorers, buccaneers, and adventurers in search of the fabled land of El Dorado where houses were supposedly made of gold and roofed with silver, where precious stones paved the streets.

As she glanced across at her father sitting opposite her mouth curled into a smile. He was an unlikely-looking adventurer. In fact, with his sparse frame, stooped shoulders and slightly absentminded look he was everyone's idea of a typical professor, yet he too was a victim of Amazon madness, one of a legion of men held captive by a beautiful, alluring, secretive, yet often deadly mistress.

'I'm no expert in navigation, *senhorita*,' the student scientist chuckled. 'No matter how many times I make this journey I still find myself becoming as bemused as you seem to be by miles of monotony. No, it is this,' he tapped the watch shackling his brown wrist, 'that tells me that our arrival is imminent.'

'It was extremely good of you to undertake such a tedious journey in order to meet us at the airport,' Professor Storm acknowledged with a smile. 'My daughter and I owe you our thanks, Senhor Domingues.'

'Please call me Paulo,' the young Brazilian begged the Professor, but with his eyes upon Rebel's half-turned profile. 'No thanks are necessary, I am pleased to have been of service. And besides,' he flashed a white-toothed smile, 'I was merely carrying out my boss's orders.'

'Ah, yes,' the Professor's rather dim blue eyes lit up, 'I've heard a great deal about Senhor Luiz Manchete, and all of it good. I'm looking forward to meeting him. Tell me,' he leant forward eagerly, 'is he as knowledgeable as they say about the inhabitants of the inner Amazon? Does he really visit and converse with tribes of prehistoric head-hunters?'

'He does, Professor,' Paulo nodded assurance, his

expression suddenly solemn, 'yet he is very reticent whenever these people become the subject of conversation.'

'But why?' the Professor looked astounded. 'Surely, as one of the few white men ever to gain the confidence of savages, he should feel duty bound to share his specialised knowledge with the rest of the world?'

'I cannot say for sure,' Paulo's brow wrinkled. 'He is a difficult man to fathom—I mean no disrespect,' he assured them hastily. 'He can be stern, even autocratic, and he is never inclined to share confidences, but we would have him no other way. I can merely theorise about his reasons for keeping what knowledge he has gained about the forgotten tribes to himself.'

'And your theory is...?' the Professor urged, deeply interested.

Paulo spread out his hands in a deprecatory gesture indicating that he was merely guessing. 'The Senhor, as you know, is an official of the National Council of Amazonian Researches, an organisation founded initially to protect the Indians and to prevent white explorers from exploiting the apparently limitless riches of the forest.'

'To protect head-hunters from white men?' Rebel broke in, her voice amused. 'Surely it should be the other way around?'

'On the contrary, *senhorita*,' Paulo explained, encouraged by her interest, 'the number of Indians surviving today is only a fraction of what it was at the beginning of the sixteenth century when the first white men arrived and introduced European diseases that decimated whole tribes. Measles, for instance, is a disease most white children overcome in a matter of days, yet it is lethal to the Indian who has no immunity to the germ. Influenza is also a killer. In the light of such experience, it is easy to understand the Senhor's violent opposition to our government's policy of opening up the jungle by building a highway to assist the promotion of lumbering, mining and cattle raising. He is one of our *aristocracia*, accustomed to being heeded, yet in this instance the greed of speculators has been allowed to take precedence over the needs of the natives. The Senhor's refusal to allow strangers access into the interior of the jungle is, I believe, his own private protest against a policy with which he is in complete disagreement.'

'Then I'm afraid he will also disapprove of us,' Rebel interrupted pertly, 'because a higher authority has already sanctioned our expedition into the interior.'

Paulo hesitated, lost in admiration of the girl whose beauty had turned his head. Bemused eyes lingered upon a face fragile as a flower, blind to the determined thrust of a gently rounded chin, to the firm line adopted by a sweet mouth that seemed to him to have been especially designed for kissing, and to storm clouds gathering behind wide eyes, blue as the lone jacaranda whose blossoms supplied breathless delight to jungle travellers weary of end-

less green. But it was her coronet of blonde hair that
held him totally fascinated as he strove to imagine
the silken ropes unwound, falling in a shimmering
cascade to her waist.

When delicate nostrils arched he coloured, reminded of his manners. Swiftly he gathered his
thoughts and took up once more the thread of conversation.

'In this area there *is* no higher authority than that
of Senhor Manchete,' he boasted, bttraying a hero-
worship she found infuriating. 'Here his word is law.
To the natives, he is known as *Curupira*, which can
be translated either as "spirit of the forest" or—as
some who have suffered the lash of his anger insist—
"the wild man".'

Rebel's eyes flashed blue flame. She was not prone
to instant dislikes or to prejudging people simply on
hearsay; her father had taught her to keep an open
mind, to study carefully all that she saw, heard and
experienced before making personal observations on
any subject, including people. But in this instance her
father's advice went unheeded. Quite unintention-
ally, Paulo had portrayed the man they were about
to meet, who was to be their host and supposedly
their guide into the Amazon interior, as an autocratic king of the jungle, a man who had allowed the
power he wielded over ignorant natives to go to his
head.

'Your boss-man sounds insufferable,' she startled
the bewildered young scientist, 'but if he's expecting
from us the same meek acceptance of his decisions

that he gets from his natives then he's in for a great
surprise.

'Now, Rebel!' Her father spoke sharply. 'How
many times must I warn you to guard your impulsive
tongue? You know how much the success of this
mission means to me, I will not have it jeopardised!
Such animosity is amazing! How can you possibly
dislike a man you have not yet met? How foolish you
will look, my dear, if he should turn out to be kind,
considerate and charming, as I've no doubt he will
be. Please, Paulo, disregard my daughter's outburst,
I'm certain she will reverse her opinion completely
once she is acquainted with Senhor Manchete, don't
you . . .?'

Paulo's widening grin seemed indicative of inner
amusement, an amusement he seemed disinclined to
share because lightly he prevaricated, 'The meeting
should be . . . er . . . interesting, with surprises on both
sides, perhaps. With chemicals it is easy to decide
which two will blend and which will explode upon
contact, but with people it is more difficult. Who can
tell what impact a rebel might make upon Curupira?'

The discussion ended abruptly when the pilot indicated that he was about to land in a clearing
gouged out of the jungle below. Rebel braced in her
seat as the wheels of the plane jolted over rough
ground before finally jerking to a halt. As Paulo
helped her to the ground, her first impression was
one of stepping into a vast, luxuriant hothouse filled
with constant humid equatorial heat. From ground
level the surrounding trees achieved enormous

heights, their green canopy of foliage spread high, fighting for a share of light, leaving trunks completely bare. The interior of the forest was shrouded in forbidding darkness, starved of sunlight by its roof of leaves. Lianas thrust snake-like around tree trunks as they struggled upwards for survival and roots spread out skeletal fingers over the ground, sprawling, grabbing, stretching, as if in search of prey.

'Here come our welcoming committee,' Paulo nodded, indicating a crowd of natives hastening towards them.

Rebel willed herself not to show embarrassment as the men grew nearer. It was not by any means her first contact with native tribes, but these men seemed not merely primitive but prehistoric, naked except for streaks of red body paint. Their womenfolk, also naked, had black scrolls painted upon their bodies and bright red dye smeared over their faces and feet. But as they formed a laughing, chattering circle around their visitors it soon became clear that they had the natures of happy, uninhibited children, curious about strangers, shy, but intensely interested in anything that was new to their vast yet insular world.

Minutes later there was a roll of unseen drums and as if at a given signal a man appeared striding from a building erected on the far edge of the clearing, a figure straight and tall, as brown and unbending as the monster trees rearing to form a macabre backcloth behind him.

A devil striding out of his green hell!

Mindful of her father's warning, Rebel rejected the

uncharitable thought and schooled herself to be civil. As her father had quite rightly stated, no good could result from a show of antagonism, as the man's help was so vital to their mission it made sense to appear friendly even to the extent—her teeth gritted—of seeming impressed by his omnipotence.

'Senhor Manchete?' Eagerly her father stepped forward, his hand outstretched. 'How very pleased I am to meet you at last!'

'And I you, Professor.' The Senhor's voice held exactly the timbre Rebel had expected, deep as pools formed by swirling currents; assured as the rocks that stood sentinel along the tributaries of the mighty river; cool as spray hung like a veil over cascading falls. 'I am a great admirer of your work in the field of anthropology and have read all the excellent books you have written on the subject.'

'Why ... thank you, *senhor*!' The Professor almost stammered with pleasure. 'Coming from a man of your knowledge and experience, I consider that high praise indeed. May I introduce you to my daughter?' He half turned to beckon her forward. 'Rebel,' he presented proudly, 'this is Senhor Luiz Manchete— scientist, explorer, wild-life consultant—now engaged upon the difficult task of running an experimental tree farm right here in the forest.' He beamed upon the Brazilian. 'Senhor Manchete, meet my daughter, Rebel Storm!'

'Senhorita Storm.' She could have sworn his lips twitched at the mention of her name, but when he bowed and then raised his head there was no sign of amusement on the lean face with features so brown and sharply defined they might have been chipped from mahogany. She wanted to snatch her hand out of his sinewed grasp, but forced her fingers to remain steady, willing them not to emulate the puzzling antics of heartbeats reacting frantically to a lynx-eyed glance and swift, sabre-slash smile.

'An experimental tree farm in the middle of a forest, *senhor*?' She had intended to frame the question as a polite enquiry, but realised as soon as she saw her father's frown that her words had projected scepticism, even a trace of scorn.

It was his attitude that was to blame—mentally, she conducted her own defence; she was not vain, but neither was she used to being made to feel completely insignificant.

'Your puzzlement is understandable, *senhorita*,' coolly he brushed aside her rudeness. 'Often I find myself having to explain to outsiders why, although surrounded by timber, we are trying to grow more. The world timber markets are almost exclusively geared to soft woods, you see, but unfortunately only one tree out of every ten growing in the forest is commercially viable. It is our hope that the trees we are raising from seed will be less likely to be attacked by local diseases and parasites and that eventually our plantations will yield sufficient soft woods to interest the world's paper manufacturers. It is too soon to say whether or not our experiment will meet with success or failure, whether with modern scientific methods we will manage to tame the wilderness or whether we must resign ourselves to leaving it the way it is.'

'I'm quite certain, Senhor Manchete,' her father broke in, obviously anxious to atone for her ungracious behaviour, 'that if anyone can succeed in taming even a part of the rain forest without destroying it, that person will be you.'

Feeling illogically snubbed by the Senhor's reference to herself as an outsider, and subdued by her father's obvious displeasure, Rebel lapsed into silence as they were escorted out of the clearing and along a path through the forest that eventually led to a river bank where, set well back on a high rise, stood an impressive villa, a plantation house built of stone, with a green-tiled roof and steps leading up to a wide veranda. As they approached, a manservant wearing a spotless white coat prepared to serve drinks on low cane tables. Cane chairs with plump, colourful cushions beckoned invitingly, but when urged by their host to sit, Rebel sank wide-eyed on to a canopied couch-swing and stared around her, wondering if she had wandered on to a film set prepared for a remake of *Gone with the Wind*.

Seemingly, her father's thoughts were running along the same lines. 'Amazing!' he gasped. 'I never expected to find such style of architecture in the depths of a forest!'

'Hardly the depths,' the Senhor corrected with a smile, 'merely the fringe. There are many such houses in old Brazil,' he explained, draping his lean length across a chair. 'At one time, our country supplied most of the world with sugar. The early planters needed men to plant, cut and mill the sugar cane, but the native Indians were not much help, so they began looking elsewhere for workers. Before slavery was abolished many families were brought from the West African coast and life on the Brazilian plantation was similar to that on the cotton planatations of North America. Many of the stories of the "Old South" told by an aged Negro storyteller can be duplicated in Brazil, and similarly many wealthy planters duplicated the homes of their North American cousins.'

'Are you admitting that some of your ancestors were slave traders, *senhor*?' Rebel could not resist the dig.

'No, *senhorita*, I am not,' he slewed her a steely look. 'I cannot admit what I do not know. My family owned sugar plantations at one time, certainly, but so far as I am aware no member of my family has ever been accused of making profit out of human misery.'

It was galling the way, with a mere shrug of his shoulders, he managed to dismiss her completely. As she sipped experimentally at a tall glass of *batida*, a delicious concoction of white rum made from sugar cane, fruit juices, sugar and crushed ice, she tried to decide what it was about the Brazilian autocrat that she particularly disliked and eventually concluded that it was his aloofness, his air of godlike superiority, that was not half so evident when he was conversing with her father but which he donned like a cloak each time he addressed her.

Could it be that the Senhor Luiz Manchete was a woman-hater? Could that be the reason behind the frozen glance, the unsmiling mouth, the stiff, formal manner which, it would appear, were reserved especially for her own sex?

Her father and he were conversing easily. At the mention of tomorrow she pricked up her ears and began taking notice.

'If you feel up to it, we could set off just after sunrise on a tour of the plantation. I'm certain you will find the work we are doing interesting. But perhaps you would prefer to rest for a few days in order to recover from your long journey from England, and to give yourself time to become accustomed to the energy-sapping humidity of our climate?'

'It is thoughtful of you, *senhor*, to show such concern for my advancing years,' her father smiled, 'but I think you are forgetting that I have spent a lifetime travelling the countries of the world, consequently changes in climatic conditions do not affect me. The same applies to my daughter,' he nodded towards Rebel. 'She, poor child, has learnt to accept wherever I happen to be working as home. My dear late wife always insisting upon the family staying together. She accompanied me wherever I had to go, even when she was carrying our child, which is how our daughter came to be born in a remote area of Australia where I was studying Aboriginal tribes.

The location of her birth influenced our choice of name—Rebel is not an uncommon name in Australia, a land colonised by people so spirited they did not hesitate to speak out against anything they considered was wrong, even though, at that time, rebellion was unlawful and the punishment for such crime was exile. I must admit,' he concluded with a frown, 'that my conscience has often been plagued with the thought that I have been very selfish in depriving my daughter of a home and the sort of settled existence to which every child is entitled. Yet I console myself with the knowledge that there have been some compensations. You see, *senhor*, my daughter is an exceptionally well-travelled, extremely knowledgeable young lady, an expert in the job she has chosen to do. Without her skill as a photographer you would not have found my books half so colourful, half so informative as you claim them to be.'

Embarrassed by her father's praise, Rebel set her drink down upon a table and rose to her feet.

'I'm sure the Senhor is not interested in the story of my life, Father.' Her voice sounded sharper than she had intended. 'There's nothing so boring as a proud parent eulogising over his child.'

She regretted the impulsive reprimand the moment she glimpsed the shadow of hurt flitting across her father's face. Her lips parted to apologise, to explain that it was embarrassment and not annoyance that had put an edge on her tone.

But the Senhor's reaction was swift, cutting with contempt.

'Obviously, *senhorita*, your father was right to
worry about the gaps in your education, for if you
had been given sufficient opportunity to study the
works of Shakespeare, your famous English bard,
you would have been bound to have benefited from
his comment: *"How sharper than a serpent's tooth
it is To have a thankless child!"*'

CHAPTER TWO

THE interior of the house was a revelation to Rebel,
a monument to man's determination to transport
civilisation into the jungle. From the contents of each
room she found it possible to trace the history of the
Manchete family who, as early as the sixteenth century, had begun laying down a storeroom of trea-
sures, beginning with ivory and jade brought by explorers from the Orient; gold and gem-encrusted
goblets acquired by early colonists who had arrived
from Portugal to settle in Brazil; priceless china and
silver plate bought by wealthy sugar planters; relics
of the gold boom that had lasted for only one century, and beautiful, irreplaceable works of art she was
able to recognise as creations of Antonio Francisco
Lisboa, a famous Brazilian sculptor known the world
over as 'The Little Cripple'.

The floor of the bedroom she had been given was inlaid with deep blue azulejo tiles, and as she perched on the edge of the bed and kicked off her shoes her toes wriggled involuntarily when a delicious coolness, enjoyable as the waters of a deep, clear pool, lapped the soles of her hot feet.

The unexpected luxury of a shower beckoned from a bathroom tiled green as deep-sea depths. Everywhere, the emphasis was on coolness, everything possible had been done to shut out the oppressive, humid heat encroaching from the rain forest in the manner of a prowling beast determined to oust intruders from its terrain, only to be baulked by air-conditioning; a refrigeration plant; cool cotton bedsheets; heavy net curtains—in fact, by every comfort known to modern man.

For the first time ever, Rebel became conscious of the inadequacies of her wardrobe when she unpacked her suitcase and hung her few dresses next to an abundance of drill slacks and masculine-type shirts in the wardrobe. She had not come prepared for luxurious surroundings, nor had her father who, she remembered with a qualm, possessed only one light-coloured linen jacket that could be even loosely classed as respectable.

'Ah, well!' she shrugged, choosing the dress she considered the best of three, 'at least there'll be no female competition to shame me—one of the few compensations of living one's life in a male-dominated world!'

In the act of crossing over to the bed she pulled up

sharp, surprised by her unusual choice of words. One of the *few* advantages of living one's life in a male-dominated world?

Never in her life had she harboured doubts that she was living life exactly as she wanted it to be lived, untrammelled by possessions; unfettered by home ties, a life of freedom, independence and, most satisfying of all, large slices of adventure. The Senhor was right, she reflected soberly, she *was* an ungrateful child! She had everything a girl could possibly want, and much more than some. After all, what else *was* there except a husband, a house and babies— things as alien to her life as jungle trekking was to the average housewife!

Shaking off an uncharacteristic feeling of depression, she showered and changed into the shirtwaister dress she had chosen, barely glancing into the mirror when she had finished because she knew from constant wearing exactly how her dress would look—a plain, serviceable, washed-out blue. But she took more time over the hair that was her pride, brushing it from crown to tip with steady, even strokes, then smoothing with a silk scarf until it glistened like burnished gold. Carefully she wound heavy coils around a head that looked almost too fragile to bear their weight, then sat staring at her reflection, wishing wistfully that for just this once she could enhance her coiffure with a glittering diamond tiara.

'No use pining for the moon, my girl!' she scolded her image wryly. 'The only fine feathers that have ever come your way were the real McCoy—discards from the rump of a moulting ostrich. You'll have to rely upon charm to see you through the evening, because it's a cast-iron cert that your clothes won't get you noticed!'

But when the time arrived to make her way downstairs she was feeling much more cheerful, having convinced herself that she had been worrying unnecessarily. Experience had taught her that men who spent their time in the wilderness seldom bothered about appearances, that they found it an effort even to change into a clean shirt before eating their evening meal, much less formal attire.

Her dismay was therefore indescribable, when she sauntered towards a large *sala* from which sounds of conversation were issuing, then stood stock-still on the threshold staring horrified at a gathering of men dressed in elegant white dinner jackets, knife-creased trousers, pristine evening shirts and black bow ties, all hovering, like bees around a honeycomb, in the vicinity of a chic, stunningly attractive woman. She caught a glimpse of her father, shabby but uncaring, sipping an aperitif as he listened earnestly to his companion's conversation, before she gave in to panic and turned on her heel to flee.

'Ah! Senhorita Storm!' a hateful voice drawled while simultaneously a vice-tight grip enclosed her elbow. 'Let me get you a drink before I introduce you to members of my staff who have all been eagerly awaiting your arrival.'

Just for an instant stormy blue eyes clashed with grey, wordlessly accusing him of making her appear

exactly as she felt, a gauche, ill-dressed nobody, unused to mixing in sophisticated society. With just a
few tactful hints he could have saved her this indignity, yet deliberately he had chosen to humiliate
her as a punishment, no doubt, for refusing to bend
a knee to his authority.

As suddenly as it had appeared the urge to flee was
demolished by the heat of anger. His despicable trick
was a challenge her fiery spirit could not ignore.

'Why, thank you, *senhor*.' She pitched her tone
bright and forceful to dispel a tremble of anger. 'My
apologies if I've kept you waiting.'

She cast a brave glance around the room, nodding,
smiling at the assembled company, but actually seeing no more than a blur of anonymous faces—until
her gaze fell upon the solitary woman and encountered a vibrancy that would not be ignored, met
a look from compelling eyes transmitting surprise,
disdain, and galling amusement.

'No need to apologise, *senhorita*,' he retaliated.
'We men are quite used to the time you ladies take to
perfect your appearance.' He was openly laughing at
her now. 'First of all I must introduce you to Saffira
de Pas, the only female member of our establish-
ment.'

Increasing the pressure on her arm, he propelled
her forward.

'Saffira,' he addressed the Latin beauty with a
shapely figure cocooned in flamingo-pink lace, 'this
young woman is the daughter of Professor Storm,
whom you have already met—she, very appropri-

ately, I think, rejoices in the name of Rebel.'

'Appropriately...?' As Saffira de Pas extended a limp hand she cocked an enquiring eyebrow. 'You seem very knowledgeable on the subject of Senhorita Storm's nature, Luiz; it is not like you to pronounce split-second judgment. Am I wrong in assuming that she arrived by plane a mere couple of hours ago?'

'No, you are not wrong.' To Rebel's surprise, the Senhor sounded terse, as if sensitive not only to the criticism but also to the truth it contained. 'But Senhorita Storm's youth renders her refreshingly transparent.'

As easy to see through as a shallow pond, is what you really mean! Rebel fumed behind a mask of politely smiling composure.

'Is that so?' Saffira de Pas sounded suddenly bored. 'In which case, you will make unlikely stable mates—a wild filly and a finely-bred stallion.'

As the evening progressed Rebel discovered that the room which at first sight had seemed crowded contained, in actual fact, less than a dozen people. Dinner was a convivial affair, with conversation flowing strong and fast, and differences of opinion being aired without rancour across the length and breadth of the table.

But although she was aware that she was playing right into the hands of Luiz Manchete by appearing dull and surly, Rebel resisted all the men's attempts to draw her into conversation, remaining quiet and uncommunicative until finally they gave up and left her alone, struggling to digest the unpalatable fact that with one underhanded blow Luiz Manchete had managed to shatter her pride, her image, and her self-confidence.

Desultorily she toyed with each exotic course, unable to work up an appetite for even roast turtle eggs; duck served with a piquant juice sauce, or salad of fresh, luscious, sometimes unidentifiable fruit. All she felt was a thirst, a thirst to revenge the humiliation she had suffered—was still suffering—because of a man who, upon indecently brief acquaintance, had decided that she was in need of a swift, sharp lesson in humility.

'What exactly do you hope to discover within the Amazon, Professor Storm?' she heard Saffira de Pás question her father, who seemed to be enjoying himself immensely, quite immune to the resentments seething within his daughter.

'Information,' the Professor beamed, 'material for one of a series of books I've been writing over the years dealing with the manners and customs of primitive man. As this book is to be my last, my swan song before retirement, I should like it to be special, which is why, with the help of Senhor Manchete, I hope to make the Amazonian Indians the subject of the concluding volume.'

Rebel tensed, awaiting the refusal Paulo had implied was inevitable, only to be disconcerted by the Senhor's pleasant reply.

'It will be my privilege to help in any way I can, Professor. Whenever you are ready, I will escort you to the camps of tribes living hereabouts whose head-men can still recall many of the ancient rites that once were practised regularly but which have un-fortunately been allowed to lapse.'

She itched to interrupt, understanding perfectly the reason behind her father's worried frown. He, too, recognised that he was being *patronised*!

'Er ... that's not quite what I had in mind, *senhor*,' he corrected, mildly apologetic. 'The tribes you refer to have already been studied in depth—my aim is to visit the Indians that civilisation has not yet reached, the ones who are purported to live deep in the in-terior of the forest and exist almost in the manner of prehistoric man.'

An immediate hush fell over the company, all eyes were trained upon Luiz Manchete, whose features were masked, inscrutable as a primitive Indian wood carving.

'That will not be possible, Professor.'

Almost with relief, Rebel seized upon the Senhor's autocratic refusal as an outlet for her temper.

'Impossible is a word we do not recognise, *senhor*,' she forestalled her father's protest, 'my father and I have survived the monstrous sandstorms and water-less deserts of Turkestan; the active volcanoes and savage beasts of Africa's Rift Valley; the four-ton manta rays and vicious sharks of the Barrier Reef, the impenetrable forests and mangrove swamps of Borneo, together with countless other missions—all of which we were assured were *impossible*.'

Every presence, except that of her own and Luiz

Manchete's, receded into the background as the table between them assumed the aspect of an area cleared for combat, an arena in which Rebel waited like a lone Christian expecting to be devoured by an enraged lion.

His bite, when it came, was savage. 'And did you ever stop to think what you might be leaving in your wake, Senhorita Storm? Did it ever occur to you that the sniffle you dismissed as a trivial cold germ might have wiped out in one week tribes that had existed for centuries? Are you so selfishly self-centred, so blinded by ambition, that you refuse to respect the opinions of experts who, despite having devoted their lives to helping these unfortunate people, have recently publicly stated. "We are convinced that every time we contact a tribe we are contributing towards the destruction of the purest thing that tribe possesses".'

'Piffle!' The word exploded from her lips, cracking across the width of the table to reach the man who was spark to her tinder, flame to her dynamite. 'Primitive tribes have survived almost unimaginable odds, they have as much to give from their culture as they have to receive from ours. They can teach us much, *senhor*, impart knowledge especially beneficial to people such as yourself,' she dared to sneer, 'who dip their toes in the river of discovery and then profess to be swimmers; who posture through the jungle like actors on location, pretending to live off the land while in reality unable to exist without having orange juice and fresh lobsters flown in daily!'

A breath hissed from someone's lips and was quickly stifled. Not a hand stirred, not an eyelash blinked, as they waited tense with expectation for Luiz Manchete's reaction.

But his response was surprisingly mild, traced through with a negligent quality that contrasted sharply against the chilling glint spearing her through narrowed lids.

'Are you accusing me of cowardice, *senhorita*?'

With a stomach active as a valley of butterflies, she tilted, 'Only if you allow the criticism to rest, Senhor Manchete. If I have misjudged you, it is a simple matter for you to prove me wrong!'

Suddenly he smiled, a swift sabre-slash devoid of all amusement. 'I would not be so ungallant, *meu crianca*. It is my belief that a frustrated child should be humoured, especially one who is hungry for attention. A little girl who has never played with dolls is as deserving of pity as is a woman deprived of children.'

She was given no chance to refute his implication of immaturity. As if reacting to a signal, Saffira de Pas stood up and with an alacrity born of embarrassment, the men pushed back their chairs, left the table, and began drifting in groups towards an adjoining *sala*.

'Rebel!' She swung round to face her angry father. 'I think it's time you and I had a serious talk. The attitude you've adopted towards Senhor Manchete is intolerable—I will *not*——'

'Now, now, Professor...!' Saffira de Pas approached, sparkling with triumph, 'you must not scold your little bird for trying out her youthful wings. That contretemps was partly Luiz' fault,' she glinted, 'were he not so aggressively masculine, so very much the dominating male, impressionable young girls would not feel compelled to go to almost any lengths to be noticed. I have seen it happen so many times before,' soulfully she sighed, 'girls who, convinced that they can tame the untameable, begin by teasing the tiger, then run panic-stricken from his unsheathed claws. You will do well to remember, *senhorita*,' she advised the speechless Rebel, 'that men who know her well always refer to the Amazon as "she". The Amazon is a woman—Luiz is married to the Amazon!'

Rebel was still incredulously staring at Saffira's re-treating back, when her father's perplexed voice re-gistered upon her stunned mind.

'There are times,' he sighed, 'and this one of them, when I miss your mother terribly. I'm so sorry, my dear, I had no idea ... such a situation has never arisen before ...'

'And it hasn't arisen now!' She rounded, her eyes furiously flashing. 'Good heavens, Father, is it *really* necessary for me to deny everything that woman said? She must be a raving lunatic—a victim of Amazon madness—if she believes that I'm the least bit attracted to a devil who lords it over a green hell!'

She spun on her heel and raced out of the room, humiliated by the suspicion that Saffira da Pas was busily circulating, instilling drops of the same malicious poison into receptive ears. For some reason the Brazilian woman had taken an instant dislike to her and was turning her clash with Luiz Manchete into a weapon of ridicule, the most insidious weapon of all.

Tears sprang to her eyes and were fiercely blinked away. Living in a man's world, first as a protected child, then later as a colleague admired for her courage and her skill as a photographer, had left her ill-equipped to defend herself against the one enemy she had not so far encountered—the female of her own species, who was said to be more deadly than the male!

Without being noticed, she escaped outside on to the veranda and found the night air surprisingly cool. A moon was shining brightly, silhouetting a line of ghostly palms that were playing host to a troupe of chattering monkeys. Behind them, the indigo sky was ablaze with lightning as an awe-inspiring storm raged soundlessly in the heavens. The spectacle held her spellbound, too fascinated to notice the glow of a lighted cheroot piercing the dark void at the far end of the veranda or the figure that hesitated, then began slowly advancing towards her.

'Like the chameleon, you seek the background most suited to your nature, Senhorita Storm.'

She was jerked back to earth by the cool sarcasm and whirled like a tornado to confront her adversary.

'The same might be said of you, Senhor Manchete.' She flicked a contemptuous glance past his shoulder at the luxurious villa flooded with light, from which were issuing sounds of music, laughter, and sophisticated conversation. 'The more I see of this place, the easier I find it to understand your reluctance to abandon a life of sybaritic pleasure!'

He drew deeply upon his cheroot, so that the tip glowed fiery as a malevolent eye in the darkness. She shivered, feeling suddenly chilled, and knew that his keen, night prowler's eyes had noticed.

'It is unwise to venture out at night without a wrap. Two hours before dawn the temperature is at its lowest, making even the natives feel cold. It is then that they go down to the river to bathe, for the water, though not warm, is considerably more comfortable than the damp chill of the night air. If ever you have to spend a night in the forest, *senhorita*, be prepared to huddle close to your companions in order to keep warm.'

'You consider that hardship?' she jeered. 'I've been in many worse situations and withstood them as well as any man.'

'I believe you,' he drawled so mildly she did not immediately recognise the implied insult. 'The Amazon takes its name from a legendary race of warrior women whom the natives describe as having "pale skin and bright hair, each capable of fighting ten ordinary men". The Indians swear that such women actually exist and worship them as goddesses, but personally I can find nothing to admire about women who try to usurp man's role as hunter. Your parents were wrong to deprive you of your dolls and your playmates, *senhorita*, for constant travelling and growing up almost exclusively in the company of men has rendered you a confusing mixture of toughness and femininity. You have a beautiful body, but then so has the she-cat who prowls the jungle in search of prey. I pride myself upon being as virile as the next man,' casually he abandoned his cheroot and ground it to extinction beneath his heel, 'yet I'm certain that a night spent in your bed would not effect the slightest rise in my temperature.'

CHAPTER THREE

REBEL found her father alone when she joined him for breakfast the next morning. Although it was early, Luiz Manchete had already eaten and left the villa—she had made certain of that by watching from her bedroom window and waiting until he was some yards from the house before leaving her room.

'Luiz has just left,' her father informed her, pouring her a cup of steaming, aromatic coffee.

To have replied that she was aware of that fact would have been halfway to admitting cowardice, so instead she countered,

'Luiz...? Aren't you becoming rather too friendly with the unco-operative *senhor*?'

He nodded. 'I like the man,' he admitted frankly,

pushing a plateful of freshly-baked rolls and a silver
stand housing crystal bowls full of colourful pre-
serves in her direction. 'After giving the subject much
thought, I've decided that there is a great deal of
truth in what he says. From his point of view, our
insistence upon pursuing our own interests to the
detriment of the Indian tribes must appear very
selfish.'

She hesitated with a buttered roll halfway to her
lips. 'You're not telling me that you're prepared to
abandon your project, to leave your series of books
unfinished, simply because of one man's opposition?
It's not like you to allow yourself to become brain-
washed, Father,' she withered, fixing him with an
angry blue stare.

'No, I'm saying no such thing,' he smiled, refusing
to be rattled. 'Luiz has promised to make available
to me all the notes he's gathered up over the years
from which he assures me I'll be able to find all the
information I need about the habits, customs and
life-style of the forgotten tribes. It's second-best, I
know,' he shifted uneasily, made uncomfortable by
her baleful glare, 'but if life has taught me anything,
it's that there are times when one must compromise.
I think, my dear Rebel, that the success of the work
we've done up until now has made us both a little
conceited, a little too certain that what we were doing
would be of benefit to everyone, even the natives
upon whom we imposed ourselves as uninvited
guests.' Carefully he dabbed his mouth with a napkin

before continuing to astound her. 'I'm ready to admit that I might have been wrong, and I hope very much that you will admit the same.'

She pushed aside her plate, appalled by the realisation that her father, whose desire and enthusiasm to make his last volume a memorable one had been equal to her own, was now ready to submit to the will of an autocrat, a man so accustomed to manipulating natives that his wish was now considered jungle law.

'*You* may be prepared to take orders from Senhor Manchete, but I certainly am not! Standards must be maintained—you've always stated that my photographs are as essential to the reader as your writing, and while you may be able to work from notes, how on earth am I supposed to produce photographs without a subject? No, if Luiz Manchete won't lead me to where the action is, I must find someone else who will!'

Her father scowled, deeply displeased. 'Why must you be so wayward? If I'd suspected that you would become endowed with the qualities of your name I would have insisted upon calling you Patience, Prudence ... anything other than the unfortunately apt Rebel!'

To forestall further argument he rose from the table and began making his way towards the door.

'Ah, Professor Storm,' a cheery voice hailed him from the threshold, 'I have a message for you from Senhor Manchete. He says that he is ready now to take you on a tour of the plantations, and would you please meet him outside the stables whenever it is convenient.'

'Gladly,' the Professor snapped, brushing past Paulo with a haste that caused the young man to raise his eyebrows. 'No time could be more convenient than the present!'

'Your father seems a little out of sorts this morning,' Paulo sauntered across to Rebel. 'Is the humidity affecting him, do you think?'

'No, I am,' she confessed. 'I've annoyed him, I'm afraid.'

'Impossible!' he grinned, taking the chair her father had just vacated. 'The sight of your lovely face is sufficient to soothe any man's nerves.'

'I doubt if my father would agree with you,' she countered dryly, 'or Senhor Manchete, either. Since my arrival here I seem to have caused upset to everyone.'

'Not to me, *cara*,' he denied softly, reaching out to give her hand an encouraging squeeze. 'What you need is a little diversion, you have been cooped up indoors far too long—come, let me be the first to introduce you to some of the wonders of the forest.'

'I'd like that very much.' Her smile reminded him of sunlight dispersing early morning mist. 'Just give me a minute to fetch my camera.'

'And a light waterproof,' he called after her retreating figure. 'We are certain to have rain some time during the morning.'

As they retraced their steps along the path leading

to the clearing where the plane had landed, Paulo took her hand in his and after an initial start of surprise she accepted the gesture as a sign of friendship. Once through the clearing they plunged straight into the dimly-lighted jungle, dense with trees that had thick lianas coiled around their tall trunks.

They kept to a well-trodden path, obstructed here and there by fallen trees, some feeling soft as sponge beneath their feet, their shallow roots exposed above ground. There was very little underbrush, no rotting vegetation or dank, oppressive odour.

'How clean the forest seems!' Rebel whispered, yet the sound of her voice echoed as if in the interior of a silent, high-domed cathedral.

'*Parada!*' Paulo hissed, then froze, holding a detaining hand in front of her.

She stiffened, and felt goose pimples rising when a huge snake over twelve feet long slithered past their feet.

'Ah!' Paulo relaxed, 'it is merely a *jiboa*.'

'Merely...?' she echoed faintly.

'*Sim*,' he grinned, taking her once more by the hand to continue walking, 'a boa-constrictor, so harmless that young ones are frequently kept as house pets to dispose of rats and mice and even bats.'

'I think,' she croaked, 'I'd sooner stick to the traditional cat or dog ...'

His laughter rang out, its echo bouncing from the endless walls of silent, sullen trees. The morning air was beautifully fresh and warm compared with the almost bitter cold of the night before, and as they

proceeded farther into the brooding green jungle
Rebel began to realise that the Amazon was a world
complete in itself. Constant travelling and living in
far away places had made her a little blasée in that
she had begun to feel that there was nothing new in
the universe, no sight that she had not previously
seen, but with Paulo acting as her guide, stopping
every now and again to point out a bird-eating
spider, its long legs spanning the litter of the forest
floor, its eight eyes searching, alert for the sight of
prey; a cumbersome sloth hanging motionless from a
tree, suspended upside down by long, hook-like
claws; and a timid swamp deer raising its head from
its refuge in a tangle of bushes, she had to concede
that far from being just another jungle, the Amazon
was as different as another planet.

As Paulo guided her around a fallen tree she
stopped to photograph a clump of multi-coloured
flowers on one of its upper branches, only to start
back with surprise when as she drew nearer the
blossoms took dramatic flight, revealing themselves
as a swarm of green, white and yellow butterflies.

'You will discover that the Amazon forest is full of
such surprises,' Paulo assured her. 'It is a complete
world in itself, with its own laws, its own unique conditions, even its own seasons. Here there is no summer, autumn, winter or spring, merely wet and dry
seasons. Trees shed their leaves, buds burst into
flower, birds moult and animals breed, all at one and
the same time. After a shower of rain you will see
buds appear and be reminded of springtime, yet in

the middle of the day leaves droop and flowers die as if at the onset of autumn. Another of its contradictions is that, although the forest is luxuriant, it produces little that is edible, and in order to stay alive the Indians must wander their territory constantly searching for food.'

As if to supply proof of his words, the trees suddenly parted, disclosing a cabin in a clearing flanked by a small plantation of miserable-looking plants.

'*Mandioca*,' he told her, 'a starch-yielding plant which, together with fish, forms the basis of the *caboclos*' diet.'

When a woman appeared at the doorway of the cabin Rebel's itchy camera finger twitched. Instinctively, she aimed her camera, then with her subject set in its sights she hesitated to ask doubtfully:

'Do you think she will mind?'

'I'm sure she won't,' Paulo grinned, patting the bag slung across his shoulder, 'especially when she discovers that she is to be rewarded with a bag of precious salt.'

As they drew nearer Rebel discovered that the woman was by no means as old as she had appeared at first sight. Though her face looked tired and careworn, the flesh on her arms was firm, her brown eyes clear and her manner, when she indicated that they were welcome to step inside the cabin, was composed, completely lacking in self-pity.

While the native woman conversed with Paulo in her own tongue, Rebel snapped happily away, recording for posterity the interior of the mud floor cabin that had hammocks slung from poles, a primitive loom pushed against one wall, a litter of rough earthenware pots, and a pile of oddly shaped basketweave implements, some shallow as a sieve, others deep as a dish, whose purpose she could not fathom.

After a request from Paulo, the woman obligingly squatted upon the floor, placed one of the deep baskets between her knees, laid a flat one on top, then began rubbing pieces of dried *mandioca* root through the improvised sieve.

'After much hard work,' Paulo explained, 'she will eventually produce a coarse white substance that is their nearest equivalent to flour.'

They spent an enjoyable hour talking to the surprisingly intelligent woman who, as she shared their picnic lunch of sandwiches and coffee, explained, using Paulo as an interpreter, that her husband and children were down by the river fishing in order to supplement the food obtained from crops planted on a plot of land which in two years would become exhausted. This fact necessitated their moving on, to begin again from scratch. As they were making their farewells, she demonstrated her point by stooping to gather a handful of soil so lacking in body it trickled through her fingers as finely as sand.

When they resumed their journey through the forest Rebel voiced her puzzlement. 'What I don't understand is how the fabled El Dorado came into being, how early explorers could have recorded "royal" highways built of stone and gleaming white cities existing in the midst of jungle desert.'

'Mirages, I've no doubt,' Paulo affirmed promptly. 'No evidence has ever been found to confirm that El Dorado ever existed, neither has there been any positive proof of the existence of the legendary fair-skinned warrior women, the Amazons who gave the river its name. One must therefore conclude that the early explorers were either fantasising, hallucinating, or, getting back to my own theory, that they were seeing mirages. In parts, the river Amazon is so wide that the banks disappear from sight and islands on the far horizon appear to be suspended in mid-air. Once I could hardly believe the evidence of my own eyes when, as I was progressing by boat along a stretch of deserted river, I saw what appeared to be a huge cathedral towering over the top of a high river bank.'

Rebel's blue eyes widened at this further confirmation of the huge differences existing between this region and other uncivilised areas of the world. The Amazon was, indeed, a woman, with a woman's love of mystery, of always holding something back to encourage, enthrall, then, just as one was beginning to believe her depths had been plumbed, to inflict some further outrageous shock. It was hardly surprising that for centuries she had managed to keep men fascinated—or that one man in particular had become so dedicated to the task of ensuring her survival that any other woman, even a wife, would be looked upon as an intruder.

It was while they were sitting by the side of a clear, still pool with bushes and trees reflected upon its surface, resting their backs against the trunk of a tall palm as they watched a flock of scarlet and blue macaws fighting for fruit beneath its dark green crown, that Paulo presented a possible solution to the problem that was never far from her mind.

He had been sitting so quietly she thought he had fallen in a doze, until suddenly she felt his fingers warm against the nape of her neck and heard his husky voice groan:

'Rebel, you are so beautiful, I simply must kiss you!' Without giving her a chance to protest, he drew her head forward, then his black head blotted out the sky as he bent to steal a sweet, searching kiss from lips parted on a gasp of surprise.

His hold was firm, yet light enough to have allowed her to struggle out of reach. The choice was hers, and after a momentary hesitation she succumbed to the treacherous thought, *Here is the tool with which to further your ambition! Handled carefully, Paulo might be persuaded to transfer his loyalty from Luiz Manchete to you!*

Closing her mind to a whisper insisting that she should be ashamed to taking advantage of a boy whose emotions seemed almost as immature as her own, she offered no resistance, even managed to return the kiss which, though not unpleasant, culled not the faintest reaction from her heart, her nerves, or her ice-cool senses.

Finally he pulled away, his dark eyes shining, and with an ecstatic sigh leant back against the tree trunk with her head resting upon his shoulder, her waist encircled by his embracing arm.

Sensing that his eyes were closed, that a bemused smile was playing around his lips, she chose that moment to spearhead her attack.

'Paulo...!' she prompted in a light, drowsy tone.

'*Sim, meu amor ...?*' he enquired, contented as a petted puppy.

'... if you had to, could you find your way through the jungle to the village of the forgotten tribes?'

Luckily he was too besotted to recognise that her question was a loaded one.

'I might—if I had to,' he replied tenderly. 'Once, I accompanied the Senhor as far as the perimeter of the village, but I saw nothing, heard nothing, as I was ordered to wait there until he returned.'

'But you could find your way back there?' she urged, almost unable to contain her excitement.

'Yes ...' He hesitated as if a warning bell had rung. 'I suppose so.'

'Then please, *please*, Paulo,' she twisted round to face him so that he encountered the full blast of blue eyes blazing with hope, 'will you take me there? We could slip away quietly—just the two of us—then upon our return we could think up some convincing excuse to explain our absence. That way, I could get my pictures and no one need be any the wiser.'

Paulo knew that there were a dozen holes he could have punched in her argument, but with her lovely, pleading face so close to his own he could not think of one.

Alert to his weakening, she pressed on. 'I've enjoyed your company so much, Paulo,' she flattered, smothering a prick of conscience, 'if only you will promise to do as I ask, I'll be able to look back upon this day as one of the happiest of my life!'

'As I will also, *meu cara*,' he whispered, hypnotised by liquid blue eyes. 'If a promise from me is all that is needed to ensure your happiness, then you have it.'

'Oh, thank you, Paulo!' she cried, then had to be content with beaming her gratitude, too overcome with joy to speak.

But as silently he held her look the air became fraught with tension. Panic stirred as belatedly Rebel wondered if she had been too reckless in her eagerness to defy Luiz Manchete. Paulo was very young and immature, but he was also a Brazilian, with Latin blood running fiery in his veins.

Reprieve came suddenly in the form of a rumble of distant thunder. Wind stirred through the forest, lashing the crowns of tall trees to a frenzy. Even as they were running into the forest for shelter, the clouds burst violently open and rain fell in a solid sheet, hitting the roof of the forest with a sound like bullets ricocheting off a sheet of tin.

As they ran hand in hand along the path water poured from every leaf and branch, forming puddles that in no time at all became swollen into ponds of dark brown water inches deep. Then as suddenly as it had begun the storm ceased, and steam began rising from the floor of the forest, as if hissed from a

thousand boiling kettles. A great stillness settled, a
silence that seemed to pulsate with menace after the
tumult of the storm.

When they reached the clearing and came within
sight of the villa, Rebel's steps flagged, then halted as
she stood shivering, not because of clothes clinging
sodden to her skin, but because for some unknown
reason she had been reminded of the man the natives
called Curupira—the wild one—a name that implied
that any unwary trespasser might stumble upon a
nature possessing all the torrent and tempest, the
steaming heat and chilling menace, of a forest storm.

CHAPTER FOUR

FOR the first time in her life Rebel was experiencing
fear, fear that was a hot, dry taste in her mouth, that
was a sensation of smothering beneath a blanket of
humidity, a feeling of blood freezing in her veins
when for three nights she had shivered inside a sleeping bag that had offered sparse protection from an
incredibly chilling dampness that descended upon
the forest with the rising of the moon.

But the troublesome insects almost invisible to the
naked eye that had dined on her blood, then left as a
reminder a violent itch; the presence in the river of

teeming shoals of piranhas—dangerous fish that stripped the flesh from human bones, rendering bathing taboo; the foot-long centipedes; the alligators that floated upon the surface of the water like innocuous logs, were dangers secondary to the fear brought about by the suspicion that had grown stronger with the passing of each traumatic day that they were lost in the rain forest, that Paulo had forgotten or, indeed, had never really been certain of the proper route to take.

For the first couple of days Rebel had been too busy accustoming herself to the strange sensation of being surrounded by two things only—water and forest—to question Paulo's powers of navigation. When first they had slipped away from the plantation, their canoe laden with supplies filched, at her insistence, from Luiz Manchete's stores, he had manoeuvred confidently along the jungle river-roads, sailing straight for hours at a stretch before branching off into the first of innumerable secondary creeks and streams which he had sworn were as familiar to him as the streets of his home town.

But then, some hours ago, to her amazement and his, instead of progressing upstream the canoe had begun moving backwards, forced along by enormous pressure from a rain-swollen tributary shouldering its way to the sea. Paulo had fought desperately to maintain course, but finally, beaten by exhaustion, he had slumped down defeated and allowed the canoe to drift haywire, heaving and plunging, forward then back, until only minutes ago it had suddenly become becalmed, tossed like a twig into a backwater that was absolutely still, stagnant as a pond littered with an accumulation of leaves, twigs, blossoms, spume and dust.

'What ... what do we do now?' she croaked, and was immediately rewarded with a look bordering on dislike.

'You tell *me*,' Paulo challenged disagreeably. 'You are the expert, the knowledgeable explorer who scoffed when I attempted to point out the dangers involved in this exercise—who even hinted that cowardice was the motive behind my change of mind.'

Rebel glanced across her shoulder, made uneasy by a prickling of her scalp she felt certain was a reaction to unseen eyes. But the walls of encircling forest were broodingly still, not a leaf stirred, not a sound escaped the pressing green wilderness.

Shrugging off her misgivings, she tried to appease the humiliation of the boy who was now bitterly regretting his impulse to appear mature in her eyes.

'I'm sorry, Paulo, it's all my fault, I shouldn't have talked you into bringing me here in the first place, and it was rotten of me to goad you when, after sleeping on it, you decided you had been mad even to contemplate such a plan. Forgive me for accusing you of being chicken,' she pleaded softly, hiding her desperate fear behind a mask of calm. 'Please don't be angry with me, Paulo, I'd far rather be lost in the jungle with a friend than with an enemy!'

Even in the midst of a nightmare Rebel, in a

penitent mood, was impossible to resist.

Wiping a weary hand over a brow beaded with sweat, he relented. 'I cannot allow you to shoulder all the blame, *cara*, some of it is mine—the larger part,' he insisted when vehemently she shook her head. 'Senhor Manchete has impressed upon all of us the dangers of venturing far into the jungle without a guide. I thought,' he choked on humiliation, 'that a compass and an excellent sense of direction made me competent to trace the route he took when last we visited the Indian village, but somewhere along the line,' his head jerked upright, showing eyes miserable with shame and a kindling of fear, 'I missed the way. I have to admit, Rebel, that we are utterly and hopelessly lost, stranded in a vicious green hell that has never been known to surrender its dead.'

Though the admission merely confirmed her suspicion, she had to fight hard to combat the wave of panic that threatened to undermine her courage. Her eyes swept the tangled mass of greenery that was motionless, yet which she had begun to imagine was closing in around them, the sprawling roots inching imperceptibly nearer, the crowns of tall trees lowering menacingly, as if to exclude light and to deprive them of the very air they breathed.

'Don't be silly, Paulo,' she jerked through chattering teeth, scolding herself as well as him, 'you are allowing your imagination to run riot. The first thing we must do,' she determined, taking charge, 'is steer the canoe towards that clearing on the river bank so that we can unpack the stores and get a fire going.

I'm certain that once you have some food inside you you won't feel half so pessimistic.'

Encouraged by her brisk instructions and by the competent manner in which she supervised the clearing of the camp site to ensure that no unwelcome intruders were lurking in the underbrush; directed the stringing up of hammocks, and the swiftness with which, once he had kindled a fire, Rebel cooked a panful of porridge and sliced a tin of meat taken from their rapidly-dwindling stock of food, his young face began looking slightly less drawn, his eyes less hunted.

'You make me feel ashamed,' he confided, tucking into his meal with surprising relish, considering it formed part of a monotonous diet upon which they had existed for the past three days. 'Women are supposed to be the weaker sex, yet you have shown far more resilience to hardship than many men.'

She smiled and was about to reply when suddenly she stiffened with her fork held halfway to her mouth, listening intently.

'What is it...?' Paulo jerked nervously. 'Do you hear something?'

'Be quiet!' she snapped, pushing aside her plate in order to concentrate harder. Night had not yet fallen, so the monkeys had yet to begin their usual evening chatter, the only sound was caused by a breeze stirring through vines hanging twisted and looped from the trees, creating noises similar to the muted wheeze of a creaking, untuned organ.

Then she picked up once more the sound that had

captured her attention, an alien *phut-phut*, very faint but gradually growing stronger.

'It's a *motorboat*!' Paulo jumped to his feet to yell. 'The Senhor's motorboat! *Gracas a Deus*, he must have been following us—if only we had known that all the time we were travelling he was but a few short hours behind!'

I would have jumped into the river and risked the piranhas, Rebel decided mentally, then felt immediately ashamed of her ingratitude. Without Luiz Manchete's well-timed intervention, they would quite probably have died of starvation, exposure, or both. Nevertheless she could not help feeling, as the chugging boat drew ominously nearer, that in a very short time she would be wishing she had!

Paulo's demented yells to attract attention startled screeching birds from their perches and drew a diatribe of insults from angry monkeys who joined in the din. Even though expected, at the sight of a boat nosing into the stagnant lagoon with a tall, grim-faced figure at its helm Rebel winced, anticipating the sort of agony caused by a drill touching an exposed nerve.

Luiz Manchete's only companion was an Indian who seemed ill at ease, casting nervous glances all around him as he stepped from the boat in the wake of the other man. Rebel steeled herself for an avalanche of furious words. Even Paulo was struck dumb, rendered silent by the anger emanating from the man striding forcefully towards them.

But the quietness of his tone shocked them far more than any shout. Pinning Rebel's face with an ice-grey glare, he instructed Paulo without looking at him,

'Walk slowly to the edge of the clearing and get into the canoe. Don't attempt to speak, just do as you are told and let the Indian take you back to the plantation where you can assure Professor Storm that his daughter is no longer in any danger. Go *immediately*!' He forestalled Paulo's protest, striving to keep his voice evenly controlled, 'for if the headhunters who have been trailing you for the past few hours should decide to break cover from behind those bushes, you are almost certain to end up roasted, your body fat rendered down for use as cooking oil!'

Rebel's outraged gasp caused him not one whit of compunction, not one flicker of pity for a distress that turned her brilliant eyes dark as she watched Paulo and his Indian guide clamber into the canoe to make a swift, reluctant getaway, leaving her to the mercy of a devil in his barbarous hell.

'Sit down and finish your supper,' he ordered calmly, setting her an example by squatting by the fireside and scooping on to a plate a portion of meat and a helping of cold, unappetising porridge.

Welcoming the excuse to allow her shaking legs to collapse beneath her she followed suit, striving hard to appear unconcerned yet unable to resist darting several glances towards the concealing underbrush.

Heartened by its utter stillness, by the absence of any
staring eyes or blowpipes poking through the bushes,
she challenged him,

'I suspect, *senhor*, that this melodrama is being en-
acted as a form of punishment and that there is no
reason at all why we should not have left with Paulo
and his companion!'

Leisurely he chewed a morsel of meat and swallowed it before spelling out slowly,

'At this very moment we are being carefully
watched by an audience I estimate to be not less than
ten. They will remain watching just as long as we
stay put, but if we had all tried to leave at once they
would have pounced immediately, which is why we
must act as hostages until Paulo is clear of their
territory.'

'But you know these people, they accept you as a
friend, I've heard my father say so,' she protested
fiercely.

'Which is why, up until now, I have never tres-
passed upon that friendship,' he frosted, keeping his
movements casual, almost idle, for the benefit of unseen eyes. 'As soon as I have finished eating I will
deliver my "calling cards"—bags of salt to flavour
their food; a few trinkets for their wives, one or two
metal tools. Then a short time later I will check to
find out if my offerings have been accepted. If they
have, I'll know that my request to visit their village
has been granted, but if not ...'

His shrug made her feel cold all over.

'But haven't they always been accepted?' she queried sharply.

'Of course, up until now,' he nodded indolently, 'otherwise I would hardly be sitting here talking to you, but on each previous visit I have been alone, therefore I have no way of knowing how they will react to a stranger being introduced into their domain—and a female stranger at that. I need hardly point out to one so knowledgeable as yourself that primitive people are extremely unpredictable, one can never take their goodwill for granted—a lesson that has been learnt the hard way by many a complacent missionary who has met his Maker as part of a communal stew.'

'Cruel, sadistic brute!' she hissed across the fiery embers. 'I refuse to allow myself to be intimidated by your gross exaggerations.' As the sparkle of her defiance clashed with the flint-grey coldness of his eyes, she was vividly reminded of the night of her arrival, when she had stood on the veranda of his home watching with terrified compulsion the turmoil of an electric storm, the whirls of angry colour, the slash of lightning through grey cloud, a spectacle made all the more frightening because of its ambience of explosive silence.

'If luck should prove to be on our side, *senhorita*, we will find plenty of time to exchange insults. Time, for instance, to make plain to you my contempt of an experienced huntress who deliberately set out to seduce a young, impressionable boy in order to

render him deaf to any orders other than her own, to
blind him to the destruction of a career which, up
until your arrival, had been his first and only
priority!'

'Oh, no!' she gasped. 'You surely don't intend to
dismiss Paulo simply to get back at me?' In spite of
his warning her voice rang sharp as a pistol shot.

'I cannot spare the time to play nursemaid to any
member of my staff who is stupid enough to disregard my orders,' he scythed. 'Paulo has been
warned many times about the hazards of a jungle
housing arrow-poison frogs whose garish colours
serve to advertise possession of the world's deadliest
poison; of dangerous spiders that curl up to resemble
flower buds; of exotic blossoms with spines that
cause festering immediately they penetrate the skin!
He can hardly complain, in the circumstances, if
after having chosen to chase after a brilliant butterfly,' his glance flicked over her, 'he is left with an
unpalatable taste as a result!'

With a swiftness that indicated that his patience
was almost exhausted he rose to his feet and made
towards the motorboat, rummaging among his stores
before returning to the clearing carrying an armful
of pots and pans, a dozen or so hammers and chisels,
and strings of gaudy coloured beads looped around
one wrist. Casually he began strolling around the
perimeter of the clearing, placing items at random,
beads strung upon low branches, pots and tools posi-
tioned in a haphazard half-circle mere inches outside
of the radius of the glowing campfire.

Then, displaying an amazing immunity to fear, he resumed his seat by the fire.

Uncertain whether to feel consoled or confounded, Rebel jerked hardly, 'Are you a human being or an automaton? You may be prepared to sit there waiting for those savages to decide whether or not they're going to kill us, but I'm not! In any case, I'm beginning to doubt very much whether such savages exist, which is why I've decided to make a run for the boat —are you coming or not?' she challenged recklessly.

'Not,' he replied calmly. 'But don't let me stop you,' he disconcerted her utterly. 'Taking flight is an excellent, if somewhat drastic way, of discovering whether or not a predator is close behind you.'

She had disliked him on sight, but that feeling was mild compared with the hatred inspired by his mocking smile.

She tensed to his challenge, seeing it as both a dare and as contempt of what he obviously regarded as infantile bravado. Her toes were curling, her palms were pressing hard upon the ground for leverage, when his tightly-edged warning forestalled her intention to spring up and run.

'Before you do anything foolish, Senhorita Storm, I advise you first to take a quick glance across your shoulder.'

On the very verge of flight, her startled head spun in the direction he had indicated. She slumped back in amazement, staring wide-eyed at the empty spaces where his offerings had previously been strewn.

'You may sleep now, if you wish, *senhorita*.' She

did not realise how foolhardy she had almost been until he drew a hand across his forehead to wipe beads of cold sweat from his brow. 'We will not be expected to take up the Indians' invitation to visit their village until morning.'

CHAPTER FIVE

THE campfire had been extinguished, the hammocks rolled up and put away, the pots and plates they had used at breakfast had been washed and stored inside the motorboat that had been pulled close to the river bank and tied securely to a tree.

Luiz Manchete was busy shrouding the boat in palm fronds to camouflage and protect it, while Rebel gathered together her precious photographic equipment, preparatory to setting out into the jungle towards the head-hunters' village.

She was feeling scared and yet at the same time elated. Only the day before leaving the plantation she had been told about a native woman, one of a tribe of Indians that as a result of years of close association with whites had come to be regarded as fairly civilised, who had bludgeoned her ailing father to death in order to free him from the presence of the evil spirits she had been convinced were the cause of his illness. If such beliefs were still being held by the comparatively educated what rituals, she wondered, might they come across in a village whose occupants' life style was said to be identical to that of their descendants who had migrated from North America more than fifteen thousand years ago to become the Amazon's first inhabitants?

Her hands were shaking with excitement as she slung her bag of equipment across her shoulder and looked around for Luiz Manchete, eager for the adventure to begin, excited by the prospect of being the first one to record with the camera's eyes the manners and customs of the last remaining remnants of prehistoric man.

'Are you ready, *senhorita*?' When he strode up to her she almost smiled at him, but after a look from his cold grey eyes she substituted a brief nod. Slowly he examined her, looking, she decided, for faults in her appearance. Relieved that she had chosen to don her last remaining clean but crumpled drill shirt and matching slacks, she suffered the rake of narrowed eyes that progressed from the soft-brimmed hat of jungle green she had crammed low down upon her forehead to protect her golden hair, to the tough, serviceable shoes she had broken in years ago on many previous expeditions. She did not realise how tensely she had been waiting for his comments, until without so much as a flicker of approval he turned on his heel, sparing only a nod to indicate that she should follow.

She had imagined that the Indian village would be

situated somewhere nearby, but they struggled through the jungle for hours, stopping sometimes to slash a way through tangled underbrush, and at other times having to skirt around areas knee-deep in oozing mud. They must have covered many miles before, with a grunt of satisfaction, Luiz Manchete indicated a track beaten bare of grass by constantly tramping feet. Paying no interest to her visible determination not to complain that she was wilting in the humid heat, he pressed on until the path forked to the left, when he hesitated, his head cocked in a listening attitude.

For some seconds she could hear nothing out of the ordinary, but then her ears picked up a muted drumming noise as continuous and unchanging as a powerful heartbeat.

'Sounds interesting,' he observed briefly, shifting the position of the rifle and the bag of provisions strapped across his shoulder. When he set off in the direction of the noise Rebel followed wearily, indulging in the luxury of glaring balefully at a broad back displaying muscles writhing sinuously beneath a drill shirt dark with perspiration, clinging like a second skin. Any other man would have enquired after her well-being, would have stopped long before now for a rest, but she had no doubt that the jungle dictator was intent upon driving her until she dropped—preferably into an alligator pool!

Gritting her teeth, she plodded in his wake, too conscious of fatigue and the oppressive heat to be curious about the noise that gradually grew so loud the earth seemed to rumble beneath their feet. Her surprise and pleasure were consequently all the greater when they erupted without warning into a clearing and saw a rush of pure, virgin water falling from a height of black rock into a crystal-clear pool below.

'How beautiful!' she gasped, her tiredness forgotten. 'I simply must photograph this!' In a furore of anticipation, she began fumbling for her camera, only to be exasperated by numerous straps attached to different items of equipment that had become tangled around her neck.

'Patience, *senhorita*!' His voice sounded surprisingly tolerant. 'Water has been roaring over black rock and disappearing into clouds of its own mist since the beginning of time. This same view probably took by surprise the first human beings ever to explore the Amazon, so you can rest assured that it will still be here to photograph after we've had some refreshment, don't you agree?'

Made to feel unaccountably awkward by this first glimpse of humour, this first hint that a human being existed behind the straight, unbending trunk and stern features that seemed carved out of mahogany, she lay on her stomach at the edge of the pool dabbling her hand in the water while he shared out the flask of coffee they had saved from breakfast.

Her awkwardness was increased by the intimacy of sharing a packet of biscuits with the unfamiliarly-relaxed Brazilian who stretched his length upon a grassy bank and unbuttoned his shirt to the waist, exposing a brown torso bearing a breastplate of aggressively-black hair.

Keeping her eyes trained upon the mass of foliage floating on top of the pool, Rebel hid her nervousness behind the casual comment,

'I wonder such delicate plants manage to survive with such a force of water pounding around them.'

She heard his teeth crunch into a biscuit, then his dangerously lazy drawl. 'Such plants cannot live in any other environment, they need to be constantly bathed in river mist. In common with other delicate-looking creatures, they have proved to be a great deal tougher than they look.'

If she had had the slightest doubt that he had just made an oblique reference to herself, it would have been dispersed immediately he rolled closer, near enough to make her uneasy, but not enough to provide her with sufficient excuse to inch away. Blood began racing through her veins at a furious rate, the noise of her heartbeat pounded in her ears so that she was unable to distinguish its thud from the sound of the roaring, frothing torrent nearby. She cringed inwardly, feeling the scorch of his eyes lingering on her throat, then jerked a nervous hand upwards to clutch the plunging neckline of her shirt when his eyes travelled downward to curving, peeping breasts.

When with a subconsciously defensive action she folded her arms across her chest he laughed aloud.

'What's wrong, Senhorita Storm?' he mocked softly. 'Why do you sit so stiffly erect, why is your

face so pinched, and why do you look away whenever I try to catch your eye?'

She was tempted to blurt her mistrust of his sudden change of attitude, but hesitated, conscious that
actually there was nothing of which he could be accused. Neither vocally nor physically had he trans-
gressed. To have protested that his look was too hot
would have been to leave herself open to the charge
that the meaning behind any look could only be conjecture, a matter of personal interpretation. Why
then did she feel so hunted, so threatened by the
sheer animal virility emanating from this man whose
mocking smile made plain his lack of good inten-
tions, of his desire to punish?

Sudden insight made his motive clear. Of course!
His misreading of the situation between herself and
Paulo was behind his puzzling change of attitude!
Yesterday he had labelled her an experienced huntress; minutes ago he had implied that she was as
tough as the fragile-looking rock plants whose grip
had eaten holes in hell-black rock. Neither statement
was true. Few women had travelled as far, seen,
heard, or experienced as much as she—yet still managed to remain as naïve and as ignorant of the mysterious physical side of sex. With no mother to
instruct her, no time to read books which in any case
had not been available, and being possessed of a
father so absorbed in the evolution of man he had
failed to notice the embryo woman flowering before
his eyes, Rebel had had little choice but to remain
as innocent as the day she had been born.

But Luiz Manchete did not know that! Nor did she intend to allow such a weapon of torment to fall into his hands!

'You contradict yourself, *senhor*,' she scoffed, the crispness of her tone at variance with the jelly in her knees. 'In one breath you accuse me of being tough as a nut, and in the next you label me coy, unworldly as one of your *senhoritas* who, even today, is seldom allowed over the doorstep without a chaperone. Why should I feel shy of you?' Recklessly she faced the challenge of his probing eyes. 'After all, you are just another man, one of the many faceless travellers who have passed through my life.' She forced her eyes to remain steady, strove to maintain the enigmatic smile pinned to her lips while his grey eyes smouldered, darkened by the smoke of a damped-down fire.

'It becomes easier to understand why Paulo was so quick to fall under your influence, Senhorita Storm. Exploring is just a sideline to you, a means of providing limitless amorous adventures! I admit that at first encounter I found it hard to decide whether you were a provocative child or a scheming woman, but now I wonder no longer. A man can be forgiven for hunting game because that is challenge in its most elemental form, the sort of challenge that brought the first man down from the trees to hunt meat with his primitive wooden weapons. For most of the time man has existed on earth he has hunted to survive, but you do not have the same excuse, you hunt merely for the thrill of the chase! And yet,' the corners of his stern mouth curled into a sneer, 'I suspect that you are at heart a coward, that your success as a huntress is dependent upon a discriminating choice of game.

'Have all your victims been as young and inexperienced as Paulo? I *challenge* you, *senhorita*,' the blast of his breath felt cold against her cheek, 'to pit your wits, skill and expertise against a more formidable foe—to become a *big* game huntress! Facing danger is the height of the hunting ethic, dare to accept my challenge and discover for yourself the heady exhilaration of living life to the full by experiencing the icy clutch of danger for its own sake!'

Rebel remained stock-still, rigid as a rabbit caught by the eye of a snake, knowing that some response was expected of her, yet completely unable to formulate sense out of whirling thoughts. What exactly was he daring her to do? To pit her feminine wiles against his masculine susceptibility, her experience against his skill, to seduce his emotions as he imagined she had seduced Paulo's? He was a tiger challenging a mouse—but a proud, stubborn mouse!

Inspired by a need to save face, she managed to force a bored drawl. 'You Latin men are so emotionally predictable, so entirely devoted to impressing your masculinity upon the opposite sex. It would seem to me that, with the dangers of the jungle all around us, you would be wise to follow my example and direct your energies towards self-preservation, rather than to fritter them away in a futile and totally uninteresting battle of the sexes.'

Glad of any excuse to put space between them, she

jumped to her feet and grabbed her camera. She had
moved only a couple of steps away when his hands
descended upon her shoulders, twirling her round to
face his angry frown. Obviously, her stray words had
landed on target, rendering him angry as a prodded
puma.

'Either you are frigid or you've developed a
fiendishly clever technique to attract men's interest,'
he charged rawly. 'You leave me no alternative but
to discover for myself what is the exact truth.'

Afterwards, Rebel was never able to gauge the
exact effect his savage kiss had upon her senses.
Vaguely, during their verbal joust, she had noticed
dark clouds gathering in the only visible patch of sky,
but still she was not prepared for the deafening clap
of thunder, the scorch of lightning, the shudder of
earth moving beneath her feet that exactly coincided
with the impact of his punishing mouth.

Instinctively she threw herself close against his
hard-muscled body, her desperate fingers gouging
into his shoulders as she was tossed by the elements
and by his deliberately sensual, determinedly arous-
ing kiss. It was his tender, primitive bite into her
quivering bottom lip that pained her to her senses
and sent her jolting out of his arms.

Humiliation, drenching as the rain, washed over
her when his laughter rang out to the skies. She
tensed, digging fingernails into her palms, as she
waited to be labelled novice, only to blush deeply
when he surprised her by mocking:

'Your passion is flint that needs the shock of iron to draw its spark, *meu cara*!'

Still very much aware of the pressure of his fingers upon her delicate skin, of the exploring intimacy of his kiss, she spat:

'When passions cannot be controlled they become vices, *senhor*!'

'There is a capacity for vice in all of us,' he reminded her hardly. 'Virtue and vice are such close associates it is often difficult to separate them.'

Trembling with impotent anger, Rebel snatched her camera and stalked away, anxious to capture on film some of the unique plant forms clustered around the pool and floating on top of the water. Most species of forest vegetation seemed to have invaded the clearing—lianas searching for sunlight; plants with colourful leaves so huge they reminded her of familiar house plants gone mad; lily leaves laid flat as tea-trays upon a dark liquid backcloth lightened by an occasional floating flower; clumps of unusual fungi, some star-shaped, some prickly as cacti, others rising high on slender stalks resembling dainty, colourful parasols.

Conscious of his impatient eyes, she clicked furiously away, barely noticing in her eagerness to capture as many unique subjects as possible an irritating rash that had erupted upon her arm.

She had paused for a second to absentmindedly rub it, when he spoke across her shoulder.

'Don't scratch.' He took hold of her wrist to

examine her arm. 'What's bothering you, is it an itch or a sting?'

She shivered from his touch when he pushed up her sleeve, exposing drops of clotted blood on her skin.

'It's nothing.' When she tried to jerk away his fingers tightened around her wrist. Silently, she suffered his close scrutiny, convinced that the rash was unimportant, yet relieved when he confirmed:

'You've been bitten by the pium fly, a tiny, almost invisible pest that thrives near turbulent water. Come away from the falls.' His eyes narrowed to hide what she could have sworn was a teasing twinkle, 'In fact, it would cool both of us down if we had a swim. You'll find the far end of the pool safe, clear and deliciously cool.'

In her hot, sticky state the idea sounded too good to resist. She nodded eagerly, then hesitated, reminded of one serious drawback. 'I haven't packed a bathing suit,' she confessed sadly.

'Neither have I,' he confirmed casually, 'but surely during your years of extensive travelling you learned to accept that comfort must come before prudery?'

She had learned, and in any other circumstances she would not have hesitated to strip off and bathe in any safe spot available, but in this instance, although the pool was safe, she suspected that he was not.

And yet, she reasoned, although there was no law as such in the jungle, there did exist among explorers a code of ethics for the protection of female travellers, a code so strictly adhered to it rendered fear of unwelcome intrusion unnecessary.

'Very well,' she submitted, strangely confident that Luiz Manchete, the arrogant chauvinist, was also an honourable *fidalgo*. 'Turn aside while I undress, if you please,' she demanded primly. 'I'll shout when I'm ready.'

The water lived up to his promise. For ten glorious minutes Rebel revelled in the luxury of feeling its cool, cleansing wash over every inch of her skin. She was careful to keep her back turned upon her disturbing companion, trusting him not to steal cheating glances at her nakedness, palely visible beneath the depth of crystal clear water, and felt her faith in him was justified when, after splashing loudly for a while, he called across the width of the pool,

'Would you like to borrow my bar of soap?'

'Yes, please,' she called back gratefully, 'I'd love to wash my hair.'

The small amount of space available in the canoe in which she had set out with Paulo had necessitated taking only essential supplies, so reluctantly she had abandoned her shampoo, an omission she was now regretting.

'Fetching it across for you presents some obvious difficulties.' From the tone of his voice she guessed that he was grinning. 'To spare you embarrassment, I'll keep my eyes closed—whether you follow suit is entirely up to you!'

Hot colour rushed to her cheeks when a loud

splashing indicated that he had dived underwater and was now moving towards her. Desperately she cast around, looking for some form of protection, and with a gasp of relief grabbed a waterlily leaf, huge as a platter, floating conveniently past.

When a mahogany brown face with eyes still closed emerged dripping from the water, she held the leaf between them and peered at him across its wide, flat surface.

'You may open your eyes if you wish,' she invited, confident that her nudity was sufficiently screened.

His split-second acceptance embarrassed her, as did the chagrin she glimpsed when black, spiky lashes winged upwards.

'Sorry to disappoint you, *senhor*,' she chided stiffly. 'Obviously you read more into my invitation than was intended.'

Not one whit disconcerted, he slid the soap across the leaf towards her, his eyes making a leisurely tour of softly-rounded shoulders, lingering intently upon a cloud of golden hair tipped to copper where it dipped into the water.

Made nervous by his silent appraisal, and with the memory of his words still rankling, she snapped, 'I'm the girl who is incapable of raising your temperature, remember! Which is just as well, considering I rate you the last man in the world deserving of the privilege!'

Comforted by the thought that at last she had managed to disconcert the whip-tongued Portuguese, she lathered generously all over, then, knowing from the sound of his movements that he had left the pool and that she now had it all to herself, she swam about freely, ducking and splashing until she was completely rid of soapsuds before heaving reluctantly out of the pool.

In the act of reaching for her clothes she froze, terrified by the sight of a row of broad, ugly, barbarically-tattooed faces peering out of the bushes. It was not until they started moving menacingly towards her that she regained control of her vocal chords.

'*Luiz!*' she screamed, then ran panic-stricken towards the spot where she had last seen him.

He responded by bounding out of the bushes straight in front of her, then rocked on his heels when she cannoned into him.

'*Luiz … Luiz!*' she babbled, unaware in her terror that she was calling him by name. 'They're coming after me … over there in the bushes … a horde of vicious-looking savages!'

Comforting arms tightened around her dripping naked body, but the laughter in his voice chilled her rigid when he teased approvingly,

'You are a bedevilling enigma, *cara*. Your courage is undeniable, yet your greatest strength lies in the breathtaking appeal of your sudden bouts of feminine weakness!'

CHAPTER SIX

HEAT of humiliation dried the moisture from Rebel's body as, skulking behind the bushes where Luiz Manchete had pushed her, she fumbled into her clothes, then mustered all her courage before stepping back into the clearing.

He was standing with his back turned towards her, surrounded by naked savages, their bodies striped and spotted with body paint in crude imitations of animal markings. To her stricken eyes they looked very menacing as they crowded around him, grunting and gesticulating wildly. But he seemed quite unperturbed, was even nodding and smiling as if interpreting words of sense from their grunting babble. She hesitated, and waited unnoticed on the edge of the clearing, staring wide-eyed at men who seemed barely one step removed from animals, so far down the ladder of civilisation that the primitive tribes she and her father had encountered in past years seemed worldly by comparison.

Yet strangely, it was not the prospect of their fierce glares that set her trembling as she prepared herself for confrontation, but the deeply needling scorn of one man's amusement.

The Indians' reaction to her presence was shocking.

Immediately one of them caught sight of her his wolfish howl attracted wild looks from his companions, but as she braced for a hostile reaction they astounded her by dropping to their knees and lowering their heads to the ground, seemingly awestricken and more than a little frightened.

'What on earth...?' she appealed to Luiz Manchete, who was picking his way between prostrate bodies to reach her.

'Their actions are not so surprising.' He nodded towards the shaggy black heads lowered in deference. 'Try to imagine yourself in the position of these men who have been completely cut off from the world as we know it, separated from civilisation by miles of impenetrable jungle, living in what might almost be termed an earth-bound planet consisting entirely of trees, earth and water. Up until a few years ago, the only other living creatures they had ever encountered were the animals in the forest, which was why my own appearance was greeted with wonder and a great deal of suspicion. However, not even contact with one member of a different race was sufficient to prepare them for the sight of a creature with skin pale as milk, hair bright with captured sunshine, rising from the depths of a pool to appear in their eyes much as an angel must have appeared to the fabled people of biblical times. They see you as their own private miracle, *senhorita*,' his teak-hard features betrayed not the slightest hint of humour, 'a reincarnation of the Amazon goddess they have worshipped for centuries.'

It's just too way-out to be true! Rebel told herself as she and her companion were escorted through the forest by her band of devout worshippers.

'I can't believe it's happening!' she blurted, passing a hand over dazed eyes. 'How can I possibly live up to their image of an angel?'

'There are two kinds of angels,' he reminded her dryly. 'For both our sakes, I hope they never begin to suspect that you are one of the fallen, otherwise our visit, instead of being an interval of short duration and rare occurrence, might well terminate as did Lucifer's—in a swift and painful descent into hell!'

The natives' village was set in a ragged clearing surrounded by thick forest, communal huts shaped like upturned boats and thatched with palm leaves were scattered around a rough village 'square'. Mounds of white flour prepared from the mandioca roots were heaped outside each hut, together with odd cooking gourds, stone axes, primitive fishing rods, palmwood bows and some ugly-looking arrowheads.

As they drew near to the square a crowd of about fifty natives began gathering behind a heavily tattooed man whose profusion of stringed beads and body paint proclaimed him chief of the village. A guttural exclamation reminiscent of *'Curupira'* fell from his lips at the sight of Luiz Manchete, then he and the rest of the villagers drew back with gasps of awe when Rebel moved out of a patch of shade to contrast pale as a silver ghost against her dark-skinned, black-haired companions.

'Here we go again!' Luiz Manchete murmured under his breath. 'Try to adopt a dignified attitude if you can, and thank your lucky stars that you were born a pale-faced, blue-eyed blonde, for any other kind of female interloper would have been strung up to the nearest tree.'

Suspecting that he found the prospect not at all displeasing, she scythed sweetly:

'What's wrong, *senhor*? You're looking a trifle disgruntled. Is it because a mere female has managed to steal your thunder—you may be blind to my charms, but the natives obviously aren't!'

'Sorry to disillusion you,' he muttered, heavily sarcastic, 'but if you think these natives see you as a sex symbol then you are sadly mistaken. Their taste runs to women of huge proportions, the fatter the stronger, the stronger the better. Physically, you would appeal like a sliver of peach to a man used to gorging on melons!'

He had an uncanny ability to deflate her ego. In every battle, whether of words or looks, she came off worst, and as he led her forward to greet the village headman she found herself wishing that just for once she could be given the chance to humiliate him as she had been humiliated, to topple him from his pedestal so that he too might know what it felt like to grovel in the dust!

But his talents were amazing, she had to admit when, using the same unintelligible grunts and groans, he began communicating with the headman,

who seemed unable to tear his eyes away from
Rebel's pale, sober face.

Following Luiz Manchete's instructions, she held
herself erect and tried to look imperious, even when,
to demonstrate the great courage expected of a
leader, the headman slowly extended his hand until
his black, horny fingers were near enough to stroke
lightly across the smooth, unblemished skin of her
forearm. He jumped back as if shocked by the contact, then grunted a question to Luiz.

'What did he say?' she asked, made intensely curious by the chief's look of wonder.

'He expected his goddess to feel less substantial,'
he told her with a wicked gleam, 'but now that he
has discovered that you are flesh and blood, he wants
to know if your body is kept covered because you are
different from other women, or if your male attire is
a reminder to myself that sex with a goddess is
taboo.'

The colour that flooded her cheeks brought ex-
clamations of wonder from the watching villagers.
Intensely intrigued, they formed a close, curious
ring around her, so that the stench of bodies
anointed with animal grease assaulted her nostrils.

Involuntarily, she registered disgust by waving
them away, a gesture of disdain that had the effect of
sending them staggering backwards to fall grovel-
ling a few yards from her feet.

When the headman clapped his hands the natives
jumped to their feet and scattered inside their huts,
then emerged almost immediately, some carrying

drums, others with long pipes made of reed, and the girls and women adorned with ornate feathers and many strings of coloured, roughly cut stones.

Indicating to Rebel and Luiz that he wished them to sit, the headman squatted on the ground and when the musicians, the elderly, and the very young members of the community followed suit they took their places in a wide semi-circle. As the drums took up a throbbing beat, the men and young girls left inside the circle began to posture and prance, slow graceful movements reminiscent of ballet, then gradually their naked, sinuous bodies began writhing and swaying with the rhythm of the quickening drum-beats.

Rebel sat wide-eyed and entranced while they expressed their joy at her arrival in a form of communication that had no need of words, using the language of the dance to display their delight, their wonder and deep adoration of the goddess who had honoured them with a visit.

Bright-eyed with wonder, she glanced sideways at Luiz and was surprised to see him frowning.

'You don't seem to be enjoying the dancing, *senhor*,' she leant across to challenge.

'I'm not happy about the amount of emotional fervour they're putting into it,' he admitted slowly. 'Primitive tribes dance to express their emotional attitude towards some event they believe affects the tribe as a whole. In this instance, they would seem to be overjoyed by the addition of a great new benefactress to their ranks. According to their chant-

ing, game will now fling itself upon their arrows, fish
will leap out of the streams and there will be enough
mandioca root to supply all their needs. Even if such
benefits fail to materialise,' he assured her soberly,
'their childish philosophy will convince them that
given time their goddess will provide a miracle.'

Rebel stared, tempted to mock his theory yet
disheartened by the grimness of his expression.

'You have the unhappy knack of making me feel
nervous,' she trembled. 'Are you implying that when
we are ready to leave we might have difficulty per-
suading them to let us go?'

'Anything that has a bearing upon their food
supply is of paramount importance,' he explained
laconically. 'Although the forest looks amazingly
luxuriant, because of the poverty of the soil the
natives have to work hard to scratch a living, all they
can manage is a few straggly fields of mandioca,
blowsy palms and banana plants, and a little cotton
and tobacco. Luck, to them, is a few extra fish, and
to catch a bush turkey is great good fortune, so can
you wonder that they are a people riddled with superstition, who treat every unusual happening as a good
omen, when the mainstay of their survival is hope.'

By the time the dancers had exhausted themselves
and their watchers night had fallen and fires had
been kindled under cooking pots set outside of the
malocas, living quarters housing three to four families each.

Indicating that he wished them to follow him, the
chief led the way across the clearing, then pointed

proudly to a brand new *maloca* in the final stage of construction.

Inside, a young native girl was knotting cotton thread around strands of palm leaf fibre, finishing off a pair of hammocks, one of which had already been slung from poles directly overhead.

'Do you prefer to sleep in the top or the bottom hammock?' Luiz enquired in a lazy drawl, enjoying the rush of embarrassment colouring her cheeks. 'In order to be spared the discomfort of sharing a hut with the village bachelors who sleep so tightly packed together on the floor that when one rolls over the rest must follow, I intimated to the chief that you are my woman, but to avoid detracting from your status I explained that a goddess who assumes human form naturally inherits all of a human's appetites, which reasoning they seemed to find quite logical.'

'No doubt they would,' she scathed, 'having minds that are childishly simple, but you will find it much more difficult to talk me into sharing a hut with you! If you don't fancy dossing down with the natives, then take a blanket and sleep in the bush.'

He waited until the chief had made his departure and they were alone inside the hut before reproaching with mock sorrow:

'Would you leave me to the mercy of the snakes, the centipedes, and the ants that can turn an animal into a skeleton in a matter of minutes?'

Rebel shuddered from the reminder of the day she and Paulo had been unfortunate enough to set up camp in the path of marching ants. A faint hissing sound had been the first intimation of their presence before they had sighted the advancing army, millions of tiny bodies unrolling like a carpet upon the floor of the forest, searching every leaf and twig for food, turning the plates and pans black with bodies before advancing onwards, leaving the utensils scoured, depleted of every particle of porridge, every tiny biscuit crumb.

But he was playing on her sympathies! He was a seasoned traveller, too jealous of his comforts to step into such a trap.

'Find yourself an anteater!' she suggested tersely, pacing nervously around the hut.

Disorientated by almost total darkness, she misjudged his position and stumbled into his clutches, caught like a rabbit in a trap.

'Heartless little wretch!' Merciless hands gripped her shoulders. 'What are you afraid of?' He shook her hard. 'Of retribution? Afraid that the day of reckoning has finally arrived and you cannot run for protection beneath the paternal wing? You have my word, *senhorita*, that you need fear no danger from me—not even if we were sharing a bed, much less two separate hammocks!'

But her panic-stricken senses would not believe him, not when the intimacy of his kiss still burned her lips, not when his aggressive masculinity was filling every inch of the dark, secluded sleeping place.

But he seemed determined to stay! She could not eject him forcibly, and there was no one she could turn to, *unless* ...!

Immediately the thought presented itself she acted upon it. Running to the doorway of the hut, she shouted as loudly as she was able in the direction of the camp fires where she could just make out shadowy groups of natives.

'Help me, please help me ...!'

The language of a feminine plea is universal. In seconds the natives were crowding around, looking from her to Luiz, who had simultaneously appeared in the doorway.

Stretching to her full, slender height, Rebel pointed an accusing finger in his direction, then gestured to the natives to take him away.

'Why, you devious young devil...!' Angrily, he began striding towards her, his expression thunderous, only to be cheated of revenge by a spearhead tipped with curare pointed menacingly at his throat.

'At last, *senhor*,' she sparkled triumphantly, 'I've found a way to repay you for your arrogance, for your ragbag of insults and most of all, for the amorous trick you played in order to pay me back for the way in which you *imagined* I'd treated Paulo!'

But five minutes alone inside the pitch dark hut was sufficient to convince her that she had been very, very foolish. She sat perched on the edge of the hammock, trying not to listen to the rustling of loosely-thatched walls; a nameless sighing; frogs large as puppies croaking in the nearby river; a birdcall rending the darkness, and most worrying of all, the enormous outer ring of silence which, as she concentrated, seemed gradually to magnify.

In one respect, Luiz Manchete had been right, she *was* missing her father's company. For the first time in her life she was alone in a place far more dangerous than any they had played at exploring—for compared with this experience their travelling had been a game, a game of pleasure with very little danger attached. The reality of the Amazon had turned out to be far more dramatic than she had imagined!

As she swung in the hammock, marooned in a pit of darkness, she felt she was sinking deeper and deeper into a strange wilderness, that she would be swallowed without trace and never be heard of again. A rustling noise caused her to raise her foot nervously from the floor. Was it a snake charging a venomous course towards her? Hysteria gripped her. What a fool she had been to deliver Luiz Manchete into the hands of unpredictable savages. What if they should harm him, *kill him, maybe*!

Such a thought had not occurred to her. A scream choked in her throat as she jumped from the hammock, all other perils forgotten, and ran towards the door. Outside was a still void of silence with not even the dying embers of camp fires to lighten the darkness. Almost sobbing with fear, she began running in the direction of the village square, her dilated eyes so unseeing she missed the dark patch of shadow that veered towards her, then clutched her by the shoulders when she would have sped past. A hand whipped across her mouth, stifling the scream on her lips, then a blessedly familiar voice whispered in her ear.

'For heaven's sake, keep quiet! It's only me, Luiz ... in any case, why are you running amok out here?'

'*Luiz* ...!' she gasped, making no attempt to hide her fear or the trembling that was shaking her like an ague from head to foot. 'I was afraid the natives might hurt you ... it didn't occur to me when I played that silly trick! Oh, Luiz, I'm so pleased they've set you free!'

She sensed his hesitation, heard his gasp of surprise, then was suddenly plucked from her feet and lifted close to his rock-hard chest.

'There really was no need for you to feel so afraid,' he comforted sternly, striding towards the hut looming out of the darkness. 'Working on the premise that husbands and wives act out the same sort of scenes all the world over, I explained to the natives that our spat was no more than a lovers' tiff, and they proved my guess to be correct by actually urging me to try my luck once again. I'm glad I took their advice, *cara*. Men know so little about women,' he admitted with a sigh, 'small wonder that the female gender has been applied to the Amazon, for she too can both fascinate and aggravate, invigorate and deflate, provoke, excite, tease and tantalise, then, when man thinks he knows her well, can confound with a complete reversal of character.'

He strode inside the hut, his night-prowler's eyes pinpointing the hammock without difficulty, then after laying her gently inside it he stepped back to urge, 'Sleep well, young Amazon—man's greatest confusion ...'

CHAPTER SEVEN

THE day had opened fresh as an uncurled leaf, but Rebel had waited until late afternoon when the sun's rays were just beginning to slant, before taking her camera and setting off towards the river. She had meant to go alone, but as she was leaving the hut Luiz Manchete came striding towards her from the direction of the village square.

'Where are you going?' He eyed the collection of photographic equipment strung about her person.

'There is one particular shot I want to take of the river, and at this time of day the light is just about right,' she explained, put on the defensive by his stern look reminding her that he had ordered her never to stray from the village alone.

But in place of the reprimand she had expected, he fell into step beside her. 'I'll come with you,' he surprised her by saying. 'I've often studied the colour plates in your father's books, wondering at the skill of a photographer capable of capturing her subject with such dramatic effect—one can almost feel the sting of spray, the movement of the wind. Some of your photographs are so uniquely beautiful I could never tire of looking at them. You may have drawbacks as a traveller, *senhorita*, but they are superbly compensated by your skill as a photographer. If you will permit me, I should like to study your technique. I promise not to get in your way.'

'Of course,' she stammered, confounded by the flow of praise from a man whose respect, up until now, had been as lacking as water from a dry river-bed. 'You won't disturb me,' she assured him shyly, even though the cast of his shadow was sufficient to set her nerves tingling. 'In fact, I must warn you that once I find a suitable subject I become immersed in my work to the exclusion of everything around me.'

As they made their way through the dense green tunnel of jungle, she was surprised to discover that he was keenly interested and quite knowledgeable about her work. Her shyness completely disappeared as she concentrated upon giving lucid and informative replies to his questions.

'Although a subject may look beautiful,' she explained, 'it doesn't always follow that it will result in a beautiful picture. A great deal depends upon the photographer's use of his camera. This afternoon, for instance, I should like to take a shot that will give a fleeting impression of falling water glimpsed through dappled leaves, but in order to achieve a delicate effect I must first carefully organise the framing so that the shape of the waterfall is complemented by the foreground leaves—this also helps with the problem of composing a shot when there's movement across the frame.'

'How do you avoid the error of allowing the foreground leaves to overwhelm the subject?' he queried.

'By framing with the utmost care, and also the exposure is crucial; a slow shutter speed blurs the moving water, while the rocks and foliage stay sharp. Because of the correspondingly small aperture, this more than anything is the secret of bringing a scene to life. Many of my favourite pictures have been shot with a multiple exposure, and by using such a method I've managed to retain both detail and a feeling of movement—leaves appearing to dance upon a tree; flowers seeming to bend and sway in breeze-tossed grass. That is the method I intend to employ this afternoon,' she confided, patting a collapsible tripod slung from her shoulder. 'The shot I'm after is in a heavily-shaded area where there is just not enough light to freeze the motion of the water and have enough depth of field for the shot, therefore I'll try a series of short exposures which I'm hoping will build up the light yet still result in a sharp image.'

Suddenly aware of how vociferous she had become, she broke off to apologise with a blush, 'You must excuse my running on like that—there's nothing more boring than having to listen to a poet reciting her own verses.'

'What a bundle of contradictions you are,' he scolded mildly. 'On the one hand, a banner-waving, drum-beating champion of foolhardy causes, and on the other, a secret well of intelligence and serene capability. You have much in common with the Amazon, *senhorita*, a river which because of its erratically flowing tributaries is never twice the same.'

In spite of his strange comparison, the afternoon developed into one of the most enjoyable Rebel had ever spent. With his reassuring presence at her side, it became easy to admire the violent beauty of their surroundings and to ignore the ever-present threat of danger, the suspicion that brightly-plumaged birds soaring overhead might any minute swoop to peck out one's eyes, or that given the chance, fish drifting lazily through the water might strip the flesh from one's bones.

When the heat of the afternoon grew oppressive they halted for a while. Luiz cleared a small space on the ground near the river, making certain that it was of free of ants before collecting an armful of broad wild banana leaves which he spread as a make-shift groundsheet.

For a while they sat silent, drinking in the stillness which, after close observation, revealed frantic acti-vity—leaves heaving above a stirring lizard; twigs quivering beneath the weight of a prowling spider; the languid flight of brilliant blue and black butter-flies; the groan of heavy fruit drooping from the trees then the occasional plop when one, overburdened by ripeness, detached itself and fell from a giddy height into the water.

Rebel was startled out of her reverie by a howl that reverberated around the forest and left echoes bouncing from the solid wall of trees.

'Just a monkey warning would-be intruders to keep out of its territory,' Luiz explained, amused by her wide-eyed look of enquiry.

She tilted her head, trying to trace the source of the noise that had seemed to come from directly overhead, but the closely matted canopy of leaves remained still and unstirring.

'Are there no large animals in the forest?' she queried, suddenly realising that the only creatures she had so far glimpsed had been insects, birds and a few small reptiles.

'Very few,' he replied, 'and those that do exist are so widely scattered one rarely catches sight of them. Which is why the Indians seldom dine on fresh meat. The reason for the scarcity of animals is simply that there is not sufficient food to support them, the only ones that have survived are those that have adapted to the peculiar conditions of the region by making their homes high up in the rain forest canopy, or along the river banks where light and food are concentrated.'

'You mean most of them live up there?' She peered upward to the forest ceiling and was rewarded by the sight of a troupe of acrobatic monkeys swinging from branch to branch, then dangling by their tails, heads downward, greedily stuffing bananas into their mouths.

'*Sim*,' he nodded, 'even the jaguar and the puma who are more at home on the ground and are rarely seen by day. At night time the jungle reverberates with the roars of big cats setting off on the prowl. But for how much longer, I often wonder ...?' Rebel was startled by the sudden bite in his voice, and by the hardness of his expression when morosely he continued, 'In a pitifully short space of time, just like the Indians, they will be displaced, harassed, then ultimately destroyed by man's encroachment.'

Her breath caught in a gasp as she studied the effect his thoughts were having upon the teak-tough man whose sinewed body had tensed as if poised for combat, whose eyes, grey as leaden skies, betrayed an electric flash that seemed to warn of a built-up storm.

Curupira! Up until that moment she had considered the title too dramatic for the aloof, cool-mannered *senhor* who kept a tight rein upon his emotions, but now that she could sense the force of his inner anger, the strength of his regard for the inhabitants of this unique area, she began dimly to realise that given sufficient cause, and with passions sufficiently inflamed, Luiz Manchete might merit his title of the wild man!

'You consider the onset of civilisation to be more of a threat than a benefit?' she sympathised, then held her breath, prepared for an explosion of wrath.

But the steady evenness of his reply held even more impact. 'It is a tragedy, no less,' he told her simply, 'a crime against the only simple form of humanity left remaining in this over-materialistic world. Simply to satisfy man's lust for wealth the Amazon is being raped, stripped of her purity, her most precious and secret places defiled by the greedy hands of prospectors, lumberjacks and thousands of pioneer farmers misled by promotional literature full of blurb implying that because the forest is luxuriant it will produce equally luxuriant crops. But the rain forest will never be suitable for agriculture,' he clamped, 'as has been proved many times over by the Indians who have been farming in the forest for many thousand of years with pitiful results. Nevertheless, the destruction continues, bulldozers and jeeps mangle and chew the undergrowth, thousands of miles of forest have been cut down and burnt by men who refuse to accept that the Amazon cannot be tamed, that she would prefer to die rather than to submit to the indignity of bondage!'

Rebel stared wordlessly, envying the Amazon her passionate lover, wondering rather wistfully how any flesh and blood woman could hope to compete for the affections of a man so deeply committed, so utterly possessed by his flamboyant mistress.

'You refer to the Amazon as if it were a woman— the only woman you have ever loved,' she faltered.

His flashing smile sent her heart soaring to the tree tops. 'A beloved object that I am in danger of losing,' he admitted gravely, 'which is why I am grateful that the results of your work will help to preserve her memory.'

By the time she had taken sufficient shots of the scene she had set out to capture, the sky was darkening and a wind had blown up, causing the air to grow chilly. Yet when Luiz suggested it was time to turn back she pleaded, her ears attuned to the sound of crashing water, 'May we continue just a little farther—I think I hear falls nearby?'

To her relief he made no objection, but indicated a

canoe anchored to a tree on the river bank. 'We might as well make use of this,' his good-humoured smile showed sympathy for her objective, 'it looks rather primitive, but it's perfectly safe, providing you remember not to rock the boat.'

Metaphorically speaking, Rebel had no wish to rock the boat, for during the pleasant, totally compatible afternoon, their relationship seemed to have progressed from out of the rapids and into a haven of calm waters. Once or twice he had quite naturally called her Rebel and once, with a dry mouth and frantic heartbeats, she had managed to utter his name. His unstinting praise, his genuine show of interest in her work, had smoothed salve on to her wounded pride so that now even the squirm-inducing memory of running naked into his arms had become blurred, as had the awful ache she had felt since the first time he had insisted that he had no interest in her as a woman.

As a man she found him very interesting indeed. For the first time in her life she had begun equating all sorts of terrifying, exhilarating, confusing and deeply sensitive emotions with being in the company of one of the opposite sex. For a girl who had been deprived of the opportunity even to play such childish games as 'doctors and nurses' or 'mothers and fathers', who all during her teens had had her father ever present to ensure that she was treated as a child, sister, niece or even granddaughter by their male travelling companions, it had been difficult to conclude that she was in love—in love with a man who on more than one occasion had expressed his complete indifference!

Nevertheless, when they rounded a bend in the river and saw volumes of water crashing down from a ledge on to jagged rocks below the world seemed to her to be more wonderful than ever before, much bigger, more brightly-coloured and infinitely more interesting. Her happiness must have been reflected in her sparkling eyes, for when she turned her head away from the view to search for her camera she met his quickened glance and felt suffused by a warm, happy glow.

'Row a little nearer to the torrent,' she begged, her hands shaking with excitement as she focused her camera upon the rush of dark, cloud shadowed water pierced by a burst of dying sunlight. She began snapping feverishly, anxious to record the scene from every angle before the weak ray of sunshine faded.

'Be careful, Rebel!' Luiz' shout of warning came too late to prevent her from leaning at an angle too acute for the safety of the cockleshell boat. Even as he yelled the canoe overturned, precipitating them both into a rock-pierced cauldron of seething water.

Rebel's one thought, as she tumbled into its icy grip, was for the safety of her camera. Desperately she strained one arm upward to its fullest extent, holding the camera above water as she struck out with the other towards the encouragingly-close river bank. But when a rough hand grabbed her shoulder she relaxed and floated like a sapling on the surface while Luiz towed her into the shallows.

She had sunk only one small footprint into oozing mud when his anger exploded.

'*Imbecil! Grande idiota!* How could you endanger your own life for the sake of a replaceable object! If I had not reached you in time, would the last I saw of you have been a hand clutching a camera?'

Sodden hair plastered black as thunderclouds above glowering eyes added macabre emphasis to his rage as he stood towering, outraged as a jungle cat with his sleek pelt dripping. This fleeting comparison was too much for Rebel's sense of humour. Laughter began as a muted murmur in the well of her throat, then rose to burst from her lips in a surge of helpless merriment.

The louder she laughed, the deeper he glowered, until finally her aching sides could stand the strain no longer. 'Oh, Luiz!' she spluttered, 'I'm sorry if I gave you a fright, but there's no need to look so indignant—after all,' she gulped, 'all you've suffered is a ducking!'

Her jeer was like spark to dynamite. She had an instant impression of smouldering eyes, then earth, sky, trees and water exploded around her when she was grabbed and shaken so vigorously she felt her head was in danger of snapping from her shoulders.

The rapport she had cherished disappeared immediately, devoured by the heat of his anger and by the flare of her furious resentment.

'Have you no sense of humour, *senhor*?' she spat across the dividing yard of space she had fought to put between them. 'Are you too conscious of your role of proud *fidalgo*, of conquering conquistador, to appreciate a joke at your own expense? You have lived too long among easily-impressed natives!' she flung, rubbing her tender shoulders to erase pain inflicted by the grip of his fingers. 'You *need* to be ridiculed occasionally, if only to remind you that in the country of the blind the one-eyed man is king!'

'Just as you, *senhorita*, need to be reminded to act in the manner expected of a woman, instead of like a tomboy who prefers trousers to skirts and has an irritating tendency to copy the behaviour of a reckless adolescent!'

She fought hard to fight back tears of hurt. With hindsight, she realised that her action had been foolhardy, that she ought to have reacted immediately to his warning instead of allowing her absorption in her work to take precedence. Yet even so, the strength of his reaction was completely out of proportion to her small crime, for after all, he was as much aware as she that most predators lurked in the deeper, murkier stretches of river and were seldom found in shallow rapids. She had to conclude that it was the unexpected ducking that had upset the decorum of the dignified *senhor*.

Perhaps if she had been named Prudence she would have hesitated to sneer, but as it was she had the honour of generations of Rebels to uphold, a legion of courageous namesakes who had suffered imprisonment, deprivation and exile in their fight against injustice.

'All men should practise endurance!' she scoffed contemptuously.

'Just as all women should learn how to cry!'

She sensed the devil on his shoulder mere seconds too late to avoid the savage crush of arms that pinned her tight as a slender liana to a rigid tree trunk. She might, in time, have forgiven the outrage of his kiss if only it had been a sweet salutation instead of being bitter with the resentment of a man goaded against his will, aggravated by the knowledge that he was doing wrong and by his inability to prevent it.

Forces of revulsion and response warred within her body as she quivered beneath the experienced touch of a man who was no stranger to secret places, a seasoned traveller of unexplored territory, determined, forceful, intent upon gaining ground.

Then, as she was fighting the wicked languor stealing across her body in the wake of his caressing hands, as she struggled to rise above the tide of passion aroused by his storming kisses, she felt a shudder rack his frame, heard a breath rasp deeply in his throat, and realised with sudden clarity that their roles had become reversed. The knowledge brought relief and a heady sense of elation that pushed her to the brink of surrender. *He loved her!* He wanted her, not merely to prove his superiority nor to demonstrate mastery, but because he could no longer help himself!

Uttering a small cry of tenderness, she melted close

and pressed shy lips against his hard mouth. But with a gasp that was almost a snarl he pushed her away.

'*Meu Dios, senhorita!* You surprise me, I did not expect my challenge to be taken up with such alacrity! First I am favoured with an exhibition of nakedness to whet my appetite, followed by a display of physical hunger calculated to undermine any man's immunity. For a moment I found you appealing, but then I remembered the truth men speak when they declare that there is no such thing as an unattractive woman in the depths of the jungle!'

CHAPTER EIGHT

REBEL brushed droplets of sweat from her eyes. She was making her way to the river's edge with a bundle of washing, not for the first time envying the natives their nakedness that made the chore of laundering clothes irrelevant. She had brought only one spare outfit with her into the jungle, which meant that each day because of the heavy humidity her spare shirt, cotton slacks and underwear had to be rinsed through in order to freshen up the sweat-stained material.

The exercise was never completely successful because of lack of soap—the small amount they had packed had been reserved for personal washing and by now was reduced to a carefully treasured sliver— but at least once her clothes had been rinsed and hung out to dry they felt fresher even though they looked so disreputable they would have been scorned by any self-respecting scarecrow.

Luiz ministered to his own needs, and irritated her intensely by always appearing, if not elegant, then at least comparatively presentable. Since their row a couple of days ago the atmosphere between them had remained frigid. He had moved out of the hut that night without a word of explanation, leaving Rebel to sleep alone cocooned in a dark void of rustling, creeping shadows. Because he mistrusted the Indians' standards of hygiene the ingredients of their meals were provided by him, cooked by herself, but eaten separately, therefore hardly a word had been exchanged between them since the encounter that had left her feeling bruised as a flower crushed by a thoughtless hand, a despoiled beauty with torn and ragged emotions.

Therefore she was all the more disconcerted when she dropped to her knees on the riverbank and saw him standing at the bow of a dugout canoe stirring the shallows with a long pole, searching for fish. She would have darted out of sight had not recognition been simultaneous; pride would not allow her to fall into retreat.

He had taken off his shirt and in spite of herself her eyes were held fascinated by the play of muscles beneath skin glistening almost as dark as an Indian's while he guided the canoe towards her.

'Good morning, *senhorita*.' His greeting was brief, yet immediately she sensed the absence of the attitude which during the past two days had reminded her of a cauldron simmering beneath a tightly-clamped lid.

'Hello,' she jerked awkwardly, and was struck by the foolishness of reverting to such formality in the depths of a primitive jungle.

'Would you like to help me catch some fish?' The olive branch was casually extended, making it easier to grasp.

'Yes, please ... But I'll finish washing my clothes first, if I may, so I can spread them out to dry on the bushes.'

Showing no sign of impatience, Luiz waited until she was finished, then helped her into the canoe and instructed as he handed her a basket made of palm leaf fibre, 'At the moment there is a profusion of fish in the river, consequently the natives' primitive method of fishing is showing surprisingly good results. When I stir up the shallows with this pole the fish will be frightened to the surface, so get ready to scoop them into the canoe with your basket.'

To her amazement, the method worked. At first she was awkward and too slow to retain the wriggling bodies in her scoop, but after one or two failures her persistence was rewarded when she succeeded in scooping a medium-sized fish of an unrecognisable species that brought a cry of triumph to her lips as she watched it wriggling at the bottom of the canoe.

'Is it edible, do you think?' she gasped, her shining eyes and flush of pride causing him a grin of amusement.

'Yes, it's edible, I've seen the natives eating similar ones,' he confirmed, 'but please don't ask me to name it, for the Amazon rivers are said to house over a thousand different species. Only recently, an expedition set out to take a collection of fish from specific rivers and discovered that almost fifty per cent of all they caught was new to science.'

'Then at least there's no fear of the natives going hungry,' she replied, rescuing her scoop as she prepared to improve her skill.

'Unfortunately, the catch often fails, mostly in the rainy season.' As he exerted casual strength to direct the canoe into a different patch of shallows her concentration wavered as she watched the effect of a ray of sunshine gilding his dark, tousled hair with fascinating blue glints. '... when that happens,' she forced her mind back to what he was saying, 'the Indians resort to attempting to charm the fish back by sinking a magical stone in the water, or by using the more effective method of thrashing an enclosed circle of water with poisonous vines until it is impregnated with a blue juice that numbs the fish, which then die and are scooped into baskets when they float on the surface.'

After about an hour of fruitful enjoyment, Rebel had enough fish strung on a vine to supply them

with food for the rest of that day. She was leaning
over the side of the boat, waiting with her basket at
the ready for one last attempt, when his prodding
pole caused an unusually vigorous stir in the water.
Eagerly she dug her scoop beneath the surface and
was shocked when, with a sharp imprecation, Luiz
dropped his pole and swiftly grabbed her wrist to
lever her hand out of the water.

'What on earth...!' Indignantly she glared,
shocked by the speed and forcefulness of his action.

'Look down there,' he nodded, his expression once
more grim.

Obediently she glanced in the direction he had indicated and shuddered when she saw what appeared
to be a large snake making its way through the water.
It was about six feet long, its movements sluggish
and full of evil menace.

'Ugh! It's revolting ...' she wavered.

'Shocking,' he contradicted without a trace of
humour. 'It is an electric eel. They are compensated
for poor vision by an electric sense that helps them
to navigate and to locate and stun prey. If you had
touched it you would quite probably have lost con-
sciousness from its shock.'

The equivalent of an electric current shuddered
through her frame. Suddenly the enjoyment of the
task had fled, all she wanted was to return to dry
land—to return, in fact, to the sanity of home, a home
where sparrows fed on crumbs, where flowers could
be picked without the danger of poison seeping
beneath one's skin, where the only animal noises came

from barking dogs and purring tabbies and where people lived in houses and women lived gloriously mundane lives cooking meals for their husbands and bringing up babies. *The sort of home she had never known and was never likely to know!*

Luiz accredited her intense pallor to shock, and guided the canoe swiftly towards the river bank. As he helped her ashore his glance was as sharp as his manner when he demanded:

'What's wrong, aren't you feeling well?'

She kept her head bowed, her lashes lowered over eyes she knew were reflecting the despair and agony of her thoughts. Unaware that her attitude was reminiscent of a very young penitant, she whispered huskily:

'I think our visit has served its purpose. When may we leave for home?'

He paused for so long before replying she was tempted to look up, but was glad she had not when his harsh reply scythed over her head.

'So, you have decided that what little you know about us is enough—enough to prevent you from wanting to know more! Very well, *senhorita*,' his tone sounded suddenly dry, 'I'll test the temperature of the water, so to speak, by broaching the subject to the headman. If his reaction is compliant, well and good, but if not ...!'

'You think he might object to us leaving the camp?' she trembled.

'Have you not noticed, young Goddess of the Forest,' hatefully, he reverted to mockery, 'that since your arrival the natives have enjoyed a surplus of game, and that, just as they predicted, even the manioca plants seem to be thriving?'

When they reached the village he left her to prepare their meal while he went in search of the headman. He had already cleaned and gutted the fish, so all Rebel had to do was wrap them in broad leaves and lay them on a hot, flat stone set within a circle of glowing embers, then she prepared slices of avocado pear as garnish while she waited for them to cook.

Luiz returned just as she was transferring the sizzling fish on to the large leaves they utilised as plates. He sat down and accepted his share with every sign of relish, even though the news he had to impart was disappointing.

'The headman is indisposed,' he told her briefly, applying more than half of his attention to his meal. She waited, then grew impatient when, instead of elaborating, he complimented, 'This fish tastes really good.'

She laid aside her plate, unable to agree, promising herself that once she returned to civilisation she would never choose to eat fish again. With an unconsciously weary gesture, she pushed a heavy wave of hair back from her forehead and queried:

'What do you mean by indisposed? Is the headman ill?' She knew when his sharp eyes slewed across her face that he had not missed signs of tension, an anxiety to be gone that was churning her stomach into knots.

'No, he's not ill.' His searching glance lingered on her quivering bottom lip. 'It's rather difficult to explain, but I suppose I'd better try. The headman's wife is about to give birth. It may appear fantastic to an enlightened mind, but the Indians believe that it is important that the father should pretend to play the maternal part of childbirth since he is better fitted than the mother to combat the influences of evil spirits at such a critical time. The belief prevails that the conduct of parents both before and after birth affects the child and that if, for instance, either the father or mother should eat the flesh of certain animals the characteristics of these animals will be transmitted to the infant. It goes without saying, therefore, that the flesh of the puma is highly prized, for if either parent eats it at such a time it is accepted as certain that their child will acquire the courage and ferocity of the beast.'

If he had expected her to register disbelief he was disappointed. Her blue eyes widened, her expression lightened—but excitement was the cause. Hurriedly she told him, 'I've heard my father refer to the custom as "the couvade", during which men actually mimic motherhood for a season. According to him, the word is a derivation of the French *couver*, to hatch. But such practice is not confined to the Amazon, *senhor*, for it has been known for generations that primitive fathers in many parts of the world take to their beds at the birth of a child and submit to certain restrictions of food and treatment. In some instances, the husband continues "lying in"

long after the child has been born, even though the
wife goes about her usual duties as soon as possible
after delivery. How wonderful it would be,' she
breathed, 'if I could take photographs of the "lying
in" ceremony! My father would be delighted if, in
his very last book, he could supply factual evidence
that the rumoured rite is actually still being observed!'

'I doubt if the natives would allow the presence of
even a supposed goddess at such a time,' Luiz
frowned. 'The essence of the act is for the father to
draw the attention of evil spirits by pretending to be
the mother, a weak woman prone to magical influences, so that if a devil should appear he would find
himself in combat with a strong healthy man. So
who knows what the headman's reaction might be if
you were to suddenly poke your camera under his
nose? No,' he stated decisively, putting an end to the
conversation by rising to his feet, 'I cannot allow it!
You must dismiss the thought from your mind,
senhorita, it is far too risky.'

His dictatorial command made her all the more
determined to ignore his advice, but when he left
her to stride across to the village he was not allowed
to guess that her serene expression was a mask for
scheming thoughts.

She was well aware that the lives of savages were
regulated by the principle of taboo, that at almost
every turn and especially during crucial periods in
their lives, such as birth, initiation, marriage and
death, secret ceremonies had to be observed. But

there was just a chance, she mused as she sauntered in Luiz's footsteps towards the village, that in her case the natives might be prepared to make an exception because in their eyes she was no mere mortal but a goddess, a spirit of the forest that had taken temporary human form.

With her camera slung over her shoulder she scouted around the *malocas* searching for a clue to the whereabout of the headman's retreat. Women looked up from their task of pounding, grating and sifting coconut when they heard her approach, then immediately prostrated themselves upon the ground, their naked bodies visibly quivering with awe.

Rebel sighed, wishing she had some way of communicating with them so that she might ease her own loneliness as well as their fear, but even their menfolk, brave warriors who did not hesitate to confront the vicious jaguar or the wicked-eyed puma with palmwood bows and bamboo arrows as their only form of protection, cowered from her shadow as she passed. Hoping to alleviate a little of her loneliness, she tentatively approached a young mother who was submitting her adorably chubby infant to a cool shower with water poured from a calabash shell. The infant's eyes were tightly screwed against the water streaming down his face, but he was laughing with such enjoyment Rebel involuntarily joined in. The mother's head jerked upwards, then with a look of reverential terror she grabbed her son and stumbled backwards into her hut.

Rejected on every side, and feeling more isolated

than she had ever felt before, Rebel wandered slowly on, scanning each hut as she passed but gaining no clue to the hiding place of the headman. She had almost completed her tour of the village when her attention was caught by the antics of a small boy too absorbed in his game to notice her presence. A large spider was darting on the ground around his feet. He was eyeing it keenly, judging his aim as he stood poised with a metal-tipped arrow balanced in his hand. Then suddenly he pounced and with all the triumph of a veteran hunter gazed proudly at the spider impaled upon the metal spike.

'Bravo!' she cried out without thinking, showing admiration by clapping her hands.

Instead of reacting in the same way as the others the boy puffed out his chest and beamed his delight, then, in the manner of little boys the world over, his eyes darted, searching for a further source of admiration. Inspiration sent him strutting towards a nearby hut and when he reached the threshold he looked across his shoulder as if anxious that she should follow.

Rebel pandered to his vanity by approaching close enough to peer inside and saw an interior filled with acrid smoke through which she could just distinguish a group of women kneeling beside another woman laid flat upon the ground, obviously in the last stage of childbirth.

The boy darted away, but Rebel stood rooted, fascinated by her first experience of watching a baby emerging from its mother's womb. With cries of delight the mother's helpers pounced, some ministering to the mother, the rest cleansing the new arrival, and seconds later the mystery of the smoke was explained when the infant gave a half-choked cough, protesting against his prolonged fumigation. The women responded in excited unison by uttering an unintelligible chant that Rebel had no difficulty in construing as *'There goes the devil!'*

In case her presence should cast a blight upon the happy event, she edged unnoticed out of sight, unnerved and inexplicably humbled by this close brush with motherhood, an experience that left her with a dull ache deep inside, an ache born of yearning to share the wonder and joy of combining to create life out of love.

Still in a starry-eyed daze, she made her way back to her own hut and had to drag her thoughts down to a more mundane level when she found Luiz waiting.

'Where have you been?' he rapped, his narrowed eyes questioning the purpose of the camera slung across her shoulder.

'Watching a miracle,' she replied simply, her eyes dreamy with wonder. 'I've just enjoyed the privilege of seeing the headman's wife giving birth to her baby.' His eyes pinpointed upon her softly-flushed cheeks, trembling mouth and tender, bemused expression. 'It was so wonderful,' she breathed, 'a beautiful consequence of married love.'

For some unfathomable reason his reply was grated from tight lips. 'Birth is a perfectly natural

process, *senhorita*, both animals and humans are
giving birth every second of every hour of every day.'

'How typical of you to bracket animals with
humans!' she flashed, brought suddenly down to
earth by his sneer. 'Animals copulate merely to ensure the survival of their species, whereas a human
baby is an expression of its parents' love. Scientists
are quick to label such an emotion simply as sex,
but the truth is that love is a deeper, more complex
emotion than cold, clinical men such as yourself can
ever hope to understand. As there are so few areas in
the world left unexplored, *senhor*, you might be as
well to direct your energies towards that great unknown: namely, that state of confusion known as
love.'

'I might consider doing so,' he clamped, once more
simmering on the boil, 'if you will offer yourself as a
guinea-pig so that I might investigate the everyday
chemistry of women who go crazy after man after
man!'

Rebel winced from the accusation that was becoming repetitious, an accusation that he used like a
whip to flay alive his resentment. After every enjoyable interlude, each time he suffered a momentary
weakening towards her, the charge was resurrected
even though, at times, she had glimpsed a darkening
of his expression that seemed to indicate that the
lash was causing more pain to its wielder than to its
victim.

His cruelty inspired a desire to retaliate, an urge to
make him pay for making her feel brazen, immodest,

spurned and, after his pointed reference to her
nakedness, so terribly shy of him.

'You have accused me many times of being contradictory, *senhor*,' she steeled herself to project
brazen mockery, 'yet it's becoming obvious to me
that perversity is one of your own failings. Everything you have said has indicated to me that you
despise naïveté, yet you condemn what you term my
"amorous adventures". On the one hand you label
me tough, yet on the other you imply that I'm prone
to "feminine weakness". But what I find most puzzling,' she felt her shrug of indifference was an inspired stroke of genius, 'is the way you threw down
a challenge, then when it was accepted protested at
the attack upon your immunity! What is a girl to do,
senhor,' she asked, her wide eyes deliberately innocent, 'when the big game becomes nervous of being
hunted?'

CHAPTER NINE

ALL day long drums had been throbbing a dull, insidious beat so continuous its echo had lodged inside Rebel's head, setting her temples pounding. 'It's
like a giant heartbeat,' she told herself dully, pushing a strand of hair from her damp forehead, 'the

angry pulsating of a somnolent beast prodded suddenly awake.'

The atmosphere was heavily humid, as oppressive
as that between herself and Luiz, whom she had
made very angry. All morning he had prowled, aggravated as a puma with an embedded thorn, a
thorn whose presence had been tolerable until recently when its barb had penetrated so deep it could
no longer be ignored.

'Will this noise never stop?' Irritably, Rebel addressed the back of a shirt clinging damply to powerful shoulders.

'It is not often that these people have cause to
celebrate.' He swung round to chastise her coldly.
'The drums are spreading good tidings to other tribes
in the area, telling them that after many daughters
their chief has at last been blessed with a son. They
are also sending out invitations to a feast that is to
be held this evening in honour of their white goddess, the supernatural being to whom they have
attributed the miracle.'

When he moved away as if preparing to subject
her to another day of lonely isolation, she pleaded
nervously, 'Do you mind if I join you, I'm not used
to prolonged periods of inactivity, it's driving me
mad!'

'I'm afraid that will not be possible,' he refused
with what she felt was an unwarranted degree of
satisfaction. 'The natives would be shocked at the
very thought of taking a woman on a hunting expedition—they are, of course, unaware of how

astonishingly clever you are at tracking game, how well you stick to your quarry, and how mercilessly you dispose of him once he is cornered.'

She recognised this statement as a sarcastic reference to her treatment of Paulo, the boy whom he had decided she had tracked, harassed, then finally helped to destroy.

Luiz's firm insistence that the boy's career was now at an end weighed heavily upon her mind. She had promised herself that she would plead his cause, that she would do her utmost to get the autocratic boss-man to change his mind, but instinct had warned her to wait until the time was right, to catch him in a susceptible frame of mind. Unfortunately, such an opportunity had not yet arisen.

'Too bad,' she countered lightly, trying to make her shrug appear nonchalant, then dared to conclude with the shaky query, 'The weapons of the hunt are also the weapons of war—do you see me as foe or as quarry when you direct your poisoned barbs?'

With the swiftness of a camera flash his grey eyes blazed. 'I employ poison as an antidote to disease, to render myself immune to the effects of deceit and hypocrisy that helped to cripple Paulo!'

Nursing the bitter-sweet knowledge that the extent of his dislike must at least have rendered her unforgettable, Rebel wandered through the camp with the camera she was beginning to think had become an extension of her arm, intending to take shots of the natives preparing their arrows for hunting. Though they had come to associate the clicking shut-

ter with her presence, they were still uncertain of the
black object, and though they no longer cowered
from its blinking eye their attempts to ignore its existence were patently unsuccessful. This could have
explained why they fumbled over the familiar task of
tipping poison into hollowed-out arrow shafts, fitting
a barbed metal point so loosely into the hollow that
when the arrow struck the barbed head would remain in its victim when the shaft broke away. The
poison they used was curare, which they obtained
from plants picked in the forest by the women of the
tribe, then extracted by a secret process known only
to their medicine man.

Once the hunting party set out, leaving the village
empty of all but the women and very young children,
Rebel mooched around with seeming disinterest, yet
kept an alert eye open for any clue to the where-
abouts of the chief who was not due to leave his
retreat until all protective rites had been performed
and his infant son was known to be thriving.

She hesitated, puzzled by the antics of a group of
women sitting hip to hip, forming a circle on the
ground, their trunks bent inward so that their heads
were touching as they chanted incantations and
breathed heavily upon some object that remained
tantalisingly hidden from her view. In company with
the rest of the remaining villagers she waited, and
had her curiosity rewarded when finally the women
straightened to display a mat strewn with creamy-
white lily leaves cut into strips which they proceeded
to weave into a cloak of delicate purity.

Immediately their task was finished its recipient became obvious when the women ran laughing and calling into the hut where the chief's wife had given birth to her son and emerged with the smiling mother, who submitted to being playfully pushed and tugged towards the river's edge.

Rebel felt trigger-happy by the time she had finished recording on film the purifying ceremony that was essential before the supposedly demon-ridden mother dared approach her husband. All the women of the village assembled on the river bank, then a number of them carried their chief's wife into the water where a vigorous game of splashing followed. Once back on land the women rubbed her with coconut husk fibre and coconut oil until her black body glowed smooth and glossy. Her hair was then combed and entwined with flowers before the cloak was donned—not to be discarded until the fibre had worn away and become ragged.

When Luiz returned some hours later he found Rebel engrossed in wrapping the spent reel of film in polythene to protect it from humidity and seemed to sense immediately her inner satisfaction.

'Had a busy day?' he enquired casually. 'Aren't you in danger of running out of film—you seem to have been clicking continuously since the day of our arrival?'

'I've just one shot left,' she began thoughtlessly, 'and I'm keeping that for——'

'... For what?' he prompted, eyes dangerously narrowed.

'Oh ... just for anything of interest that might crop up,' she prevaricated, annoyed with herself for almost giving away her intention. In case he should decide to begin lecturing her once again on the folly of intruding upon the headman's couvade, she headed his thoughts in a different direction. 'How was the hunting trip ... successful?'

'Very,' he replied promptly. 'Already a couple of swamp deer are turning on the spits; later tonight you can look forward to dining on venison.'

He sounded relaxed yet at the same time exhilarated, as if the excitement of the chase, the fearless courage of his savage companions had rid him of tensions and instilled fresh vigour into his veins. He exuded forceful virility from every pore, reminding her of a lustful tiger with the scent of a mate in his nostrils, when hungrily he advanced towards her.

Frightened out of her wits by his menacing mood, she backed away and took refuge from nervousness by condemning the capture of gentle creatures whose large, soulful eyes she had often seen peeping out of their refuge of tangled vegetation.

'Did you have to make sacrifices of such harmless creatures?' she croaked.

'It is the law of the jungle,' he shrugged, 'the weak must always surrender to the strong. In any case,' he shrugged, 'their days were already numbered, for we also caught the puma that was ready to attack. If your conscience troubles you, console yourself with the thought that at least our arrows spared them the agony of fangs ripping into their throats.'

Unimpressed by her shiver of revulsion, he reverted to his previous query. 'Tell me about your day —have you made much progress in your fieldwork?'

Glad of any excuse to divert his lynx-eyed look from her troubled face, she began gathering up her equipment while briefly she outlined the events leading up to the ceremony of cleansing.

'A cloak of purity!' he mocked, when she had finished describing the cloak woven with flower petals. 'How typical of woman to seek to adorn perfection! Nothing appears more beautiful to man's eyes than simple, unashamed nakedness. A loving look, a beautiful face, the sweet neglect of hair flowing free need no adornment—innocence, when clothed, is innocence no longer.'

Taking her by surprise, he moved suddenly close enough to whip an arm around her waist, lashing her tightly against his lean frame. 'What are you thinking about, sweet nymph?' he murmured, running rioting fingers through her golden hair. 'Blushing is an indication of guilt, have you been reminded of some incident of which you feel ashamed?'

'Isn't that what you intended?' she forced huskily, feeling a red-hot tide of shame mingling with an intense awareness of his vibrant body. She wanted to hide her face, to cower like a gentle doe confronted by a superior adversary, but found the courage to throw back her head, exposing the tender, vulnerable softness of her neck.

'The natives swear that a state of ecstasy often befalls one who has gazed upon a nymph,' he murmured, lowering his dark head towards her, 'a wild desire for the unattainable. Do you suppose that is why I find it impossible to blot out the memory of your enticing, petal-smooth body rising out of the water, *meu cara*? And if so, isn't it a blessing that you are one nymph who, far from being unattainable, is a self-confessed coquette who boasts of enjoying intimate familiarity with many men, a sylph who "sports and flutters in the fields of air".'

She reacted to the insult with a gasp of pain, realising, too late, how reckless she had been to taunt this pagan of the jungle, to accuse such a dangerously aggressive male of timidity.

'Please, *senhor* ...!' Without even trying he had reduced her to pleading. 'Please let me go!'

He laughed, a soft sound deep in his throat that was a mixture of half growl, half purr. Sliding his palms along her thighs, he pressed her closer. She glimpsed grey eyes dense with smouldering passion, then closed her eyes when his lips met hers in a kiss that projected the unmistakable message: *'I am all man, and I want you!'*

Trapped by the pressure of his hands, bemused by the flesh-to-flesh contact of her lips against his, she was helpless to resist a rapid rise of excitement as aggressively he manipulated her emotions, seducing her insecurity with seductive murmurings, intimate caresses and kisses which, to anyone less naïve, would have spelled out his experience in the game of sexual encounters.

When shyly she slid her arms around his neck his murmur of satisfaction should have acted as a warning, but by that time caution had been swallowed by the conviction that at last he was admitting that he loved her as much as she loved him—which was shyly, awkwardly, but with a heat of newly-awakened passion that convinced her that up until that moment she had only half lived.

They were standing entwined in each other's arms almost on the threshold of the hut, far enough away from the village to remain unobserved by any except those who might deliberately seek them out. In the grip of intense emotion, she was oblivious to everyone but the man whose kisses had brought her to life, whose caresses had injected into her veins a longing potent as a drug upon which she had become dependent, a drug whose withdrawal would set up an urgent craving. So it was left to him to voice the hoarse reminder.

'We must go inside, *cara*,' he murmured, his hands biting painfully into her waist, 'for in spite of their uninhibited attitude towards nakedness the natives live by a code of morals, a standard of behaviour, that is every bit as rigid as our own. The one thing that lovers must not on any account do, however strong their feelings, is to betray any sign of affection in public.'

Conscious that her own inhibitions were fast disappearing, she stood on tiptoe to press a tender kiss upon his faintly smiling mouth. 'How unfortunate

they are never to have learnt the art of kissing,' she
husked. 'What form of endearment do they indulge
in, do you suppose?'

'They do this.' Teasingly, he bit the lobe of her ear.
'And this!' When his fingers scratched an erotic path
along the length of her slim neck she gasped at the
impact of the pagan caress. 'So you see, they are not
so deprived after all,' he laughed softly, 'even though
their prejudice against any show of affection demands that when a couple are out together they must
not walk side by side, but one behind the other; even
though they may not hold hands, caress, or even look
at each other with love in their eyes, their restraint
is compensated by the sort of urgency that I am feeling now—an urgency to have you all to myself out of
sight of prying eyes.'

Rebel was well aware that when he swooped to lift
her into his arms and carry her inside the hut that the
last thought in his mind was to appease the propriety
of the native community. Yet once he set her down
upon her feet within the dark void of intimacy she
was unprepared for the rough haste of his fingers
fumbling with the buttons of her shirt, or for the lack
of tenderness in his voice when, impatient with his
slow rate of progress, he charged with fierce impatience:

'*Meu Deus!* One would think you were a novice—
why don't you co-operate?'

The shock of his words would not have been half
so great had he not stated on many occasions his
wholehearted approval of the high moral standards

Brazilian men expected of their brides. A strict line
divided the virtuous women from whom they selected
their wives and the 'fallen angels' who existed to give
temporary gratification. The realisation that Luiz
regarded her as one of the lower category shocked
rigidity into her limbs, froze her heated blood to ice,
so that her fingers felt stiff when she untwined them
from around his neck. Later, she was to resurrect and
examine the dull throb of anger she felt deep down
inside her, anger against the negligence of a father
who had delighted in sharing with her knowledge
gained from his lifetime study of mankind, yet who
had omitted to mention the most important fact of
all—that even after centuries of evolution the baser
animal instincts still raged rampant in the human
male! But at the moment she had more urgent prob-
lems on her mind, the problem of adjusting to being
cruelly thrust out of childhood into womanhood, the
problem of how to pacify a man's hunger—not to
love, as she had naïvely imagined, but merely to
mate.

The touch of his hands upon her cool flesh sent a
jerk of revulsion through her frame. Violently she
pulled out of his reach and had to struggle to overcome choking tears before she could speak.

'I'm sorry, Luiz,' she finally managed to gulp, 'but
I'm afraid this entire episode has been a horrible
mistake.'

She sensed him stiffen, felt angry frustration
emanating through the dark void whose ambience of
intimacy had changed suddenly to menace.

'I agree,' he clamped, 'that it is a grave mistake to lead a thirsty man to water and then forbid him to drink.'

She wanted to explain that she was no tease, that she was only now assimilating the distinction between being loved and merely making love, but she could not find words to describe the ripping away of a fragile veil of gaucherie from her eyes.

'It is rather late in the day to pretend prudery,' he charged thickly, cutting the space between them with two strides. 'Minutes ago you were melting in my arms, eager to be petted, yet now you are adopting the refinery of a cherub who has no body from the neck downwards!' Sadistic hands grabbed her shoulders to administer a violent shaking. 'I would not stoop to taking any woman against her will,' he gritted furiously, 'but for the first time ever I am able to feel sympathy for men whose frustration has driven them to savagery. Women of your type are despicable!' He released her so violently she stumbled backwards and fell in a heap on the ground. 'You may be taking comfort from the thought that one shriek for help will bring a tribe of worshippers to your aid,' he sneered, 'but bear this in mind, Senhorita Storm, I never overlook outstanding debts. Once we leave this camp we'll have four days' journey ahead of us—I guarantee that once we are alone you will not find me half so malleable as you found Paulo!'

CHAPTER TEN

All women should learn how to cry! Rebel discovered Luiz Manchete to be an excellent teacher as she lay with her tears mingling with the dust on the ground where he had left her, grappling with yet another new emotion: the pain of tears she had seldom shed throughout the even tenor of her lifetime.

But though she felt her heart was breaking, she had no regrets for the passing of uneventful years during which she had only half existed. Luiz Manchete had seduced her into glorious life, the pain she was suffering was an indivisible part of the agony of her love for him.

Because the feast the villagers were busily preparing was being held partly in her honour, she had to make an effort to prepare for it, so she bathed and changed into a fresh outfit of drill shirt and pants, then assuaged a yearning to assert her femininity by brushing her hair loose into a golden cloak that rippled past her shoulders, and copying the native girls' method of tucking a scented flower behind each ear.

Because the natives looked upon watering places as the sources of all life, as cauldrons boiling and bubbling with the creative faculty, the feast was to be

sited around the fringe of the lagoon out of which
their Goddess of Water had arisen. But in order to
repel evil spirits, flaming torches had to be carried by
the natives to guide them through the darkness where
demoniac beings swarm.

There was no sign of the headman when Rebel
took her place as guest of honour at the head of the
procession and tried not to glance sideways at the
mahogany chipped features of the man the tribe considered to be her husband. The headman's wife took
up position directly behind them, her flower-cloaked
figure looking strangely incongruous compared with
the naked simplicity of her companions.

The setting looked almost too beautiful for words
when they seated themselves in a semi-circle facing
the lagoon, its surface glowing crimson with the reflection of fiery torches stuck at intervals in the
ground, its calmness stirred only by troupes of water-
lilies swaying graceful as ballet dancers, constantly
changing formation. The music of the forest lent
muted harmony to the scene, for as if commanded,
all raucous sounds had been suspended, leaving
silence filled with the sighs of Curupira—the spirit of
the forest to whom the natives attributed all the
noises they could not explain.

As she shared a fallen tree trunk with the silent,
grim-faced Portuguese, Rebel began trembling with
nervousness, but gradually as she noted the happiness on the faces of men adorned with furs, feathers
and skins, and of girls with lissom bodies agleam

with beautifying oils, her nervousness gave way to
wonder as she experienced the curious sensation of
living in the prehistoric past, a feeling that at last she
had been accepted by the inhospitable Amazon.

But a storm was simmering inside the man seated
by her side, his tense body seemed to harness the
high-voltage anger of an Amazon storm that built up
an atmosphere of silent oppression, thunderous grey
clouds, and glaring bolts of lightning hours before
the tempest actually broke.

Finding it suddenly difficult to swallow, she
reached up a hand to ease the tightness in her throat
and gave a nervous start when his cold voice taunted:

'You share with the monkeys a fondness for fidget-
ing. I suspect that life among the primitives is not
what you expected; perhaps now you will admit that
your reckless determination to see for yourself how
the natives live was wrong—and unnecessary,' he
clipped, grey eyes swirling with storm clouds. 'Your
father could have collated all the material he needed
from my notes and from the collection I have made
of their tools and household possessions, their cos-
tumes and weapons, and a few rough items of handi-
craft.'

The contemptuous edge in his voice acted like salt
upon Rebel's smarting pride. Her trip into the interior had been as painful as he could make it, but
she would not allow him to guess that every quivering part of her was crying out that he was right.

'I don't agree,' she countered bravely. 'Museums

are crowded with collections of meaningless curiosi-
ties, but pictorial documentation helps to breathe life
into the natives' customs and life style, helps people
to appreciate their differences, to understand their
mentality, and to make them more sympathetic towards their wellbeing. Which is what you wish to
achieve, is it not...?' She tilted a rebellious chin,
daring him to deny the logic of her words. But the
argument was cut short by the arrival of native girls
bearing leaf platters laden with food—one for their
goddess whose status required that she should be
served first, and another for Curupira, whose emin-
ence was a mere fraction lower.

As she nibbled a leg of roast turkey, crisped to
black on the outside but succulently moist under-
neath, she was puzzled by the disappointed look she
saw on the face of a girl who offered Luiz the contents of a small gourd and was brusquely waved
away. She was further puzzled when the girl, instead
of offering it to herself, bowed and scurried away.

'Why wasn't I offered whatever was in the gourd?'
she asked haughtily, rendered a trifle heady by the
natives' adulation.

'*Epena* is taken only by men,' he told her dryly. 'It
is a snuff made out of mimosa seeds which dispels
aggression by producing tranquil hallucinations during which the drugged mind is filled with beautiful
visions.'

'Then I'm surprised you didn't try a pinch,' she
countered flippantly, 'you would be bound to feel the
benefit.'

He punished her for her temerity by ignoring what he knew was a reference to his simmering resentment, and reminding her silkily:

'I doubt if any drug could produce visions superior to the one I carry always in my mind of a sylphlike body, pale as milk, rising naked out of the lagoon.'

Rebel attempted to divert his mocking gaze from her fiery cheeks by lifting a gourd of fruit juice to her lips and drinking deeply.

When first she became aware of it, she imagined that the low humming sound was inside her head, a by-product of nervous tension, but as the sound increased and was joined by hand-clapping she realised that the whole tribe had joined in song to express its joyful emotions in time with the music of the drums. Above the mass of swaying bodies the feathers of the men's tall, ceremonial headdresses, each fashioned to represent a different inhabitant of the forest, quivered and fluttered, giving an almost hallucinatory impression of a mixed flock of herons, egrets, cormorants, scarlet ibises, and snow-white spoonbills fluttering above a sea of downbent heads.

Then as the drumbeats accelerated the natives' chanting grew louder, their hand clapping became more frantic, and men and girls detached themselves from the crowd to form prancing, opposing ranks. Feeling Luiz's amused scrutiny of her profile, she steeled herself to remain composed as the dancers' movements became more and more sinuous, displaying a close and obvious connection with eroticism. In a very short while she became aware that the dance was no mere form of social entertainment but an opportunity for the males to display their manly qualities, and to afford the girls a chance to show to advantage their tattooed limbs which proclaimed them eligible for marriage.

When one of the men broke off from the dance to swoop upon his partner and carry her off into the forest, Rebel's gasp betrayed her outrage.

Luiz responded with laughter strident with lack of amusement. 'I dare you to condemn the native girls as shameless,' he jeered. 'Their code of ethics forbids them to be casually provocative, the dance of court-ship demands serious commitment, and is not a flir-tatious interlude designed to drive a man to distrac-tion before they flee from the consequences.'

'Perhaps,' she defended bitterly, 'that is because they know that commitment is equally shared—that they are not merely game, creatures of the chase be-ing hunted for the beauty of their skins!'

Made to feel unbearably cornered, she jumped to her feet and ran from Luiz's leaning shadow, from the erotic atmosphere that was having the effect of a drug upon her senses, firing life into lambent desire, threatening destruction to her flimsy defences. Blinded by panic, she fled through the forest, stum-bling over roots, blundering into trees and bushes, more afraid of the hunter she sensed in close pursuit than of any perils she might encounter in the dark-ness.

Somewhere above the forest's leafy canopy a full moon was illuminating the night sky, but the floor of

the forest was dark except for intermittent patches
where moonlight penetrated holes in the leafy roof.
Rebel kept to a path she felt sure would lead her to
the village, blessing the fact that the Amazon differed
from other forests she had visited where fierce
animals lurked behind every tree and snakes were
draped from branches. Few large animals survived
for long inside the Amazon forest where the density
of the trees was an added obstacle whenever danger
threatened. Even smaller forest animals remained in
hiding until dusk made it difficult for them to be
seen. But they could be heard. Birds screeched and
called after her as she ran along the path, monkeys
chattered their annoyance at having their peace dis-
turbed.

It was not until she erupted into a small clearing
containing a peculiar-looking hut that she realised
that the path, instead of taking her towards the
village, had led her farther away. A chill of forebod-
ing prickled her skin as she noted the drawings of
animals and various other symbols painted upon the
clay walls of the hut elevated from the floor of the
forest by tree-trunk stilts, its thatched roof drooping
low over a doorway just wide enough to admit its
owner. She had not come across it before, but had
seen many like it, secret shrines of mystery and magic
where no laymen dared enter, the house of a witch
doctor, the place where he brewed his potions and
where he retreated whenever he wished to consult
the spirits.

Instinctively she backed away as she recalled the

horrifically painted face, the strangely-garbed body of the man the savages held in great awe because his clumsy conjuring tricks appealed to their simple minds as great magic. She shared their fear, because every time their paths had crossed, which mercifully had been seldom, she had sensed the witch doctor's animosity, read a message in a lip snarled upwards over blackened teeth that left her in no doubt that he did not share the natives' opinion of her female divinity.

She was just about to spin on her heel, prepared, even anxious, to face Luiz's stormy anger, when a shriek of rage, hysterical as a monkey's, rent the night air. Petrified with horror, she stood rooted to the ground watching the witch doctor's sparse frame gyrating in a dance of venom that set neck-beads clattering, head-feathers quivering, as he gesticulated his hatred from the threshold of his hut.

Like the victim of one of his magic spells, she stood frozen as he advanced upon her with menace in every step until there was less than a yard of space between them. His yells were unintelligible to her ears, but his finger jabbing incessantly in the direction of skulls impaled upon stakes surrounding his hut made plain his accusation of trespassing.

'I'm sorry ...' she gasped feebly, 'I had no intention of intruding. I lost my way ...!'

Her gibberish replies seemed to incense him to further fury. To her horror, his hand descended upon a crude dagger hanging from a belt around his waist, then as he inched forward with his hand upraised, muttering incantations beneath his breath, fear forced from her tight throat a high-pitched, terrified scream.

As if the sound delighted him he grinned and lunged towards her. She glimpsed teeth bared like fangs, felt the tug of his hand on her hair, smelled the sickening stench of his unwashed body, a mere split second before she fainted.

'*Rebel!*' The voice that pierced her subconscious was reassuring yet hoarsely unfamiliar. 'Open your eyes, *meu cara*, there's no need to be afraid, the witch doctor has gone.'

The Latin endearment touched a nerve that jerked her alive to the feel of strong arms supporting her shoulders, to the touch of tender fingers stroking her cheek. Moonlight flooded the clearing, casting a mesh of pure silver over hair spread like tangled silk across his shoulder, adding the brilliance of sapphires to eyes blazing mute relief behind lashes swept with moondust. She withstood the impact of his look just long enough to confirm that the anxious voice really did belong to the usually aggravated Portuguese, then retreated behind downswept lashes to hide the effect his concern was having upon her senses. But there was no way she could still the sweet, wild trembling that rendered her so weak she had to cling, dependent as a liana, to his tall trunk when gently he urged her to her feet.

'What am I to do with you, rebellious sprite?' he

questioned softly as a sigh against her ear. 'Am I so terrifying that you prefer the company of a jealous witch doctor to mine?'

'Jealous...?' she queried shakily, vibrantly aware of arms that once had felt steely as a trap but which were now gentle enough to nurse a newborn baby. 'Why should he feel jealous enough to want to kill me?'

Remembering the tug of his fingers in her hair, the descent of a knife in a venomous hand, she shuddered and sought strength by pressing closer to his comforting bulk. She felt him brace as if to shoulder a burden, and wondered why his voice sounded so strained when he replied.

'Because you usurped his position of authority in the tribe. Before your arrival anything and everything linked however loosely to good fortune was attributed to him, only he was possessed of mysterious powers, only he could have worked the miracle of providing the headman with a son. But you were mistaken in thinking that he intended to kill you,' he assured her, lifting a hand to clear wisps of silken hair from her brow.

'But he threatened me with a knife!' she protested, 'I saw it descending a second before I fainted. If you hadn't chased him away ...'

'But I didn't,' he contradicted with a shake of his head, 'I arrived just in time to see him running out of the clearing brandishing clippings of golden hair. Naturally,' his tone roughened, 'when I caught sight of you lying motionless on the ground I lost all interest in the witch doctor—you were my first concern.'

His face was expressionless, yet she had recognised a thread of agony running through his words and glimpsed sparks in flint-grey eyes which, had the witch doctor seen them, he would immediately have construed as portents of ill omen.

'Why did he cut off my hair?' she gasped, running trembling fingers through her shorn locks.

'Because primitive tribes believe that any shred of clothing, any intimate belonging—the cuttings of hair or nails, for example—must be carefully guarded or destroyed in such a way that there is no danger of them falling into an enemy's hands, to be used in harmful magic. Failure to observe such precautions brings a speedy penalty in its train. The victim falls ill and may—indeed, often does—die, unless steps are taken to free him from the magical influence. I have no doubt that if we were to look hard enough we would discover your hair nailed to the bark of a tree as an expression of the witch doctor's malicious intent.'

In spite of her scepticism a shiver of fear ran down her spine, as she recalled her father discussing with some of his colleagues the inexplicable death of an Australian aborigine whose shadow had been stabbed by an enemy.

Fully aware that she was giving in to illogical superstition, she croaked, 'What are the precautions that have to be observed?'

To her relief he did not mock her naïveté, but consoled grimly, 'Such things are best left to the natives. Once his reckless act has been brought to their attention, they will seek to curtail any further activity on his part by killing him and then driving a stake through his corpse to prevent his malignant spirit from wandering. But don't worry,' he hastened to appease her wide-eyed horror, 'it is my guess that once the witch doctor has had time to reflect upon his folly he will decide to put miles between himself and the tribe whose goddess he has offended.'

He remained deep in thoughtful silence as they retraced their steps, skirting the lagoon where the drug-dazed natives were still feasting and revelling, until finally, without encountering a soul, they entered the deserted village.

Not until they were outside her hut did he break his silence. 'After giving the matter some thought, I've decided that we must leave the camp at dawn tomorrow. The natives will take hours to sleep off the effects of the *epena*, and when they do so, and discover that you have departed as suddenly as you arrived, they might in time be persuaded that your presence was hallucinatory, that you were merely a figment of an *epena*-induced dream. That way, I'll be able to retain their trust, and be certain of a welcome when I return on one of my periodic visits to check up on their wellbeing. See to it that all your gear is packed,' he ordered, taking her consent for granted. 'I want you to be ready to leave shortly before sunrise.'

But sunrise was still long, fear-filled hours away,

hours she would have to spend alone inside the darkened hut with only the memory of the witch doctor's evil, hate-contorted features to keep her company. The thought drove her to an act of desperation which in other circumstances would have been unthinkable. Lulled into complacency by his show of concern, and eager to demonstrate her gratitude, she stood on tiptoe to surprise him with a shy kiss.

'Couldn't you stay with me for the rest of tonight?' she pleaded.

Hard hands descended upon her shoulders to push her away.

'Never do that again!' he clipped harshly. 'I do not possess the strength of Hercules, *senhorita*, although there are times when you make me feel I'm sharing part of his burden—he too had a tunic forced upon him which, when he tried to remove it, he discovered was stuck fast to his skin!'

CHAPTER ELEVEN

A COUPLE of hours later, although her pride was still smarting, Rebel had the events of the evening in clearer perspective. As she groped around the hut, gathering up her scattered equipment, she almost

laughed aloud as she reflected upon her spurious fear
of the witch doctor's mumbo-jumbo. 'The man is a
fakir,' she told herself, 'a clumsy conjuror who's
terrified of having his secrets revealed!'

But unknown to him, one of his secrets *had* been
revealed, for while she had been packing her gear
ready for departure her memory had clicked with
the split-second action of a camera shutter, bringing
to the fore the last thing her mind had photographed
immediately before she had fainted.

Excitement welled up inside her as she mulled
over the resurrected cameo: a moonlit clearing; a
barbaric hut starkly outlined against a background
of trees; the witch doctor's face looming in the foreground with, beyond his upraised arm, a glimpse of
the headman's terrified face peering round the doorway!

She had one flashbulb left—an essential requisite
if her camera was to penetrate the shroud of darkness hiding the secrets of the *couvade*. There were
also two hours left before dawn—ample time for her
to get to the witch doctor's hut and back again with
the coveted photograph in her camera. The more she
pondered the stronger her instinct grew that the
opportunity should not be missed. All signs seemed
to be pointing in her favour. The witch doctor, Luiz
had assured her, would be miles away by now; the
natives were completely absorbed in their merry-
making, and she had two long hours to fill before the
time of their departure. Why should she not put them
to good use, and delight her father by providing him

with proof of a ritual which up until now had been damned by sceptics as mere conjecture?

Her father had often accused her of wilful stubbornness, and as she crept through the forest gripping her camera in a trembling hand it crossed her mind that what she was doing might have struck him as very foolish. Luiz would be furious if ever he found out, but now that she had memorised the way, the witch doctor's hut did not seem as far distant, so she felt confident that she would have ample time to take her photograph and return to the village before he had even noticed her absence.

The headman's reaction to the sudden brilliance of the flashbulb was her main worry. Would he accept it as part of her magic, or would his primitive mind immediately associate its intrusion with harm to his newborn son? Consoling herself with the thought that he was hardly likely to connect evil with the goddess whose magic he was convinced had helped him to produce an heir, she pressed on with lightened spirits, passed the now-silent lagoon where the natives lay sprawled among silent drums and the debris of the feast, asleep on the ground where they had dropped, the women exhausted from dancing, the men overcome by the effects of the *epena* drug.

The clearing when she reached it was ghostly still, no fluttering wings to set leaves rustling, no padding of small paws to disturb the underbrush. It was as if even the animal world had accepted that this place was taboo, forbidden territory to all but the witch doctor and his haunted spirits.

Cautiously, her heart thumping fast as a frightened bird, she set one foot upon the rope ladder and began the short climb upwards to the wooden platform stretching the length of the hut. No creak betrayed her as she tiptoed towards the open doorway, aimed her camera at the darkened interior, then snapped her shot.

The scene revealed by the blinding flash of light was to remain stamped upon her memory for ever, as was the barbaric screech of rage that burst from the throat of the headman, who was lying in his hammock, painted jet black from head to foot, wearing a wig of long hair crudely arranged to resemble his wife's hairstyle, and having strung around his neck, wrists and ankles many feminine baubles filched from his wife in order to trick evil spirits into thinking that they were dealing with a weak woman susceptible to their spells, rather than her strong warrior husband.

The same flash that rendered the headman temporarily blinded also inflicted upon her the shocked realisation that she had seriously blundered. She had owed the strength of her assurance to the conviction that the headman would recognise her as a friend, but while the light had illuminated the hut she had remained in the shadows, giving him the impression that he was being attacked by an invisible enemy!

Sensibly, she did not wait to reason with the gibbering headman, but without waiting to reveal herself she ran, half tumbling down the rope ladder in her haste to get away. She was halfway across the clearing before she became conscious of heavy rain. Storm clouds had gathered and one of the downpours that were a daily occurrence in the rain forest had begun lashing the branches of trees, flattening the underbrush, reducing paths to quagmire.

She had cause to bless the timing of the elements when, just a startling second after the moon was blacked out with the speed of a snuffed candle, a spear thudded into the earth at her feet. Rigidity shocked through her limbs as the quivering shank brushed her shoulder. Impelled by the instinct to survive, she sped a weaving, panicking course towards the sheltering trees. It could not have taken her more than a few seconds to cover the open ground, yet she felt she had spent an agonising hour evading spears aimed with the uncanny accuracy of a hunter whose game was his livelihood, before she stumbled behind a barricade of trees and raced swift as a demented deer, holding her hands over her ears to shut out the sound of the headman's screams of demented fury.

Unaware of whether or not he was following, and too terrified to stop to find out, she continued running as fast as the darkness would allow, blundering into tree trunks that loomed too suddenly to be avoided; tripping over roots that sent her thudding to the ground with a force that knocked the breath from her body; falling headlong into underbrush, frightening screams from small animals whose reactions were no less startled than her own; slipping on wet paths, splashing through puddles, but all the time sheltering her camera as best she could from the teeming rain.

The scene that greeted her when she stumbled inside her hut seemed a fitting climax to the horrific episode. Standing in the middle of the floor she saw Luiz with a flaming torch in his hand, obviously about to set out in search of her.

'Where the devil have you been?'

She stood rooted, staring with the shocked look of a hunted animal who, after gaining the safety of its lair, discovers that it has blundered into a trap. She remained speechless, too stunned even to search for words as Luiz's incredulous eyes scoured slowly downwards from hair that was a sodden, mud-streaked mass, cheeks oozing blood from crisscrossed thorn scratches, and clothes plastered to her body like a second skin, except where contact with the prickly underbrush had torn jagged rents. Then his needle-sharp glance veered, drawn like a magnet in the direction of hands she had instinctively thrust behind her back.

'What are you hiding?' he asked, his tone pitched dangerously soft, threateningly even.

'I ... nothing ...' she stammered, then gulped, agonised as a child caught out in a lie.

A forceful hand was extended towards her, palm uppermost. 'Show me...!' he demanded, less lightly. 'I should like to examine the *nothing* that is so unimportant it brings panic to your eyes.'

Aware that the game was up, she slumped, then

with a dejected sigh withdrew her hand from behind her back and silently handed him the camera.

For a second Luiz looked blank, at a loss to understand to what use she could put a camera on a pitch-black, stormy night. Then, displaying a train of expression ranging from incredulity to amazed disbelief, he finally reached a conclusion.

'You implied that you had a particular reason for reserving your last shot of film,' he accused levelly, seeming too confounded to believe the words his lips were framing, 'but even if you had somehow managed to discover the secret of the headman's hideout, not even you would be stupid enough to return to the witch doctor's hut ... with your camera ... to intrude upon the ceremony of the couvade?'

The silence that followed his stunned question was woven heavily with her guilt and his simmering anger, then, following the pattern of chemicals wrongly mated, the aftermath was explosive.

'*But you did, didn't you?*' Enraged fingers gouged into the soft flesh of her shoulders as he vented his frustration by inflicting a thorough shaking. Without a whimper Rebel withstood the storm that broke over her head, the thunderous scowls, the lightning flashes of scorn, the built-up voltage of violence that erupted in a hail of stinging, lashing words. 'Are you so simple-minded that you have not yet realised that these people are savages, *head-hunters*, so removed from civilisation they do not hesitate to slay their enemies, who even indulge in the repulsive practice of eating their dead? You dare to shudder from my touch,' he lashed, 'yet your stupidity has exposed us both to the danger of being either roasted alive or hung from a tree until our bones are dry enough to be reduced to a powder, then mashed with banana to be eaten as a macabre dessert!'

His diatribe was calculated to shock, yet a little of his anger faded when her stricken face paled whiter than lily petals that floated about the lagoon like miniature ice floes.

'Don't...!' she gasped. 'I'm sorry, I realise now that I was wrong to do what I did, but please, Luiz, stop it. I can't bear to hear any more ...!'

In a passion of terrified remorse she collapsed against him racked with hoarse, gulping sobs. For a minute or so he allowed her the tension-relieving luxury of tears before curtly commanding:

'We've no more time to waste, I'll allow you five minutes to change into some dry clothes, then we must leave immediately.'

Rebel dared not protest that the flaming torch was an invasion of privacy as she fumbled with buttons that seemed suddenly to have enlarged to twice the size of their buttonholes, and barely had time to register relief at his thoughtfulness in turning his back until she had shrugged her chilled body inside a set of dry clothes.

By the time he had hooked his rifle and the knapsacks containing their belongings across his shoulders she was dressed and waiting with her precious camera clutched tightly in her hand. Luiz's nod of approval was so unexpected she was almost reduced to tears, but she forced them back and listened intently to his instructions.

'Follow behind me as closely and as quietly as you can. Our only chance of survival lies with the motor launch, we must reach it and get out of this tribe's territory with the minimum of delay. Ready...?' he queried sharply, preparing to extinguish the torch.

'Ready,' she quavered.

'Good!' To her fevered imagination his mouth seemed almost on the verge of a smile. 'Then let's go.'

The rain had ceased, the moon was once more riding high in the heavens as they began picking their way through the forest, taking care to tread soundlessly, avoiding bushes whose rustling leaves might have betrayed their intention to escape. As they skirted the perimeter of the lagoon they saw, by the light of dying torches, that the natives had not yet roused out of their drugged sleep. Rebel's heart seemed to be beating a frantic tattoo in her throat as, following Luiz's mimed plea for extra caution, she tiptoed in his wake until they had left behind them the lagoon she was always to associate with her first experience of acute fear, acute embarrassment, and acute awareness of one man's virile magnetism.

Once they froze in their tracks when they heard a violent crashing through the underbrush ahead. It might have been the headman engaged in a demented search for his attacker, or perhaps a large animal, one of the lynx-eyed puma that prowled at night in search of food. but whichever it was Luiz was taking no chances. He waited until the sound had faded into the distance, then unhooked his rifle from his shoulder and held it at the ready while cautiously they progressed forward.

Not until the village was about two miles distant did he relax and swing the rifle back across his shoulder. In the moonlight his profile seemed etched out of teak as she trembled in his elongated shadow, expecting a fresh outburst of hail from the storm she sensed still simmering behind hooded lids. But his words, when he spoke, lacked heat, fell light as summer rain.

'For the time being, I think we can consider ourselves safe. The tribes in this area are constantly warring, so the headman will not venture this far away from the village without an escort of warriors. Rest a while,' he flung a knapsack down upon the sodden earth. 'Five minutes, no more,' he reminded her when she sank with obvious relief on to the improvised seat. 'Once daylight breaks the natives will be able to track us as easily as they track game, which is why we must try to reach the motor launch before dawn.'

'But we don't know for certain whether the headman recognised me!' she reasoned desperately. 'In fact, the more I think of it, the more certain I am that he was blinded by the flash. Even as I ran across the clearing the moon was obscured by cloud, so I suspect his spears were flung indiscriminately, not at any visible target.'

She heard the hiss of his indrawn breath, saw the muscles of his forearm knot like ropes, but to her relief after seconds of taut silence he decided to ignore whichever remark had provoked his anger and continued in a tone that struck her as strangely unsteady.

'Your supposition may be correct, but on the other hand it may not. In the circumstances we dare not hang around to find out, for even if the headman did fail to recognise you, the tribe will not relinquish their goddess without a fight. They see you as a legend come to life, as an omen of good luck, a provider of peace and plenty.'

His derisory laughter jolted far worse than the headman's spear. A plea for agreement threaded her words when shakenly she charged:

'I can't profess to be Dame Fortune, but surely there must have been times ... odd occasions,' she swallowed hard and forced herself to go on, 'when my company was not too disadvantageous?'

She was thinking of the times, precious to herself, when they had chatted companionably, enjoyed serious discussions, had even laughed together at the discovery that they shared the same sense of humour, so she was not prepared for the bitterness of Luiz's reply.

With a suddenness that was frightening, he reached out to jerk her close to his hard, angry body. 'There is no advantage to be gained from the company of a miser,' he condemned thickly. 'A woman who deals out her favours in small parcels, making it easier to scoop them back again. Fasting makes a man greedy, *cara*, and as every gourmet knows, a good meal ought to begin with hunger!'

When his starved mouth descended upon hers every pulse in her body leapt in response to his urgent physical need. Many times she had daydreamed, imagining what it would be like to engage in the natural expression of the overwhelming love she felt for him. She longed for unity, to become part of his mind, part of his body, perhaps in time even to be allowed a glimpse of his soul. The impulse to communicate her love physically was equal to his, but in spite of her eagerness, in spite of a weak, boneless body and clamouring pulses, she hesitated, paying heed to a small voice warning that he was in no way committed.

A rush of revulsion sent her tearing out of arms that had become complacent, certain of victory.

'There is an understanding among travellers, *senhor*,' she charged bleakly, 'an unwritten law that imposes upon men a duty to ensure that any female companion is allowed to travel unmolested!'

His proud head jerked as if from a blow and for the first time ever she saw dull colour rising beneath his skin. The aristocrat's pride was in revolt, his honour crying out to be defended!

'I beg your pardon, *senhorita*, it was certainly not my intention to *molest*, but merely to supply the sort of diversion ladies enjoy—even expect. If I have offended you, I am sorry, nevertheless, in fairness to

myself I must point out that hypocrites who live
more than one life cannot complain if they are made
to die more than one death!'

CHAPTER TWELVE

REBEL was staggering with exhaustion by the time
the sun's warm fingers began penetrating the layer
of cold air that shrouded the forest each evening. As
she reeled in the wake of the man whose capacity for
inflicting punishment seemed endless, her weary
mind was struck by the fanciful notion that the whole
forest seemed to be weeping—every branch, trunk
and stem wreathed in mist, every leaf drooping
heavy with rainbow-shot beads that rolled over their
surface to career with a plop over the edge, setting
up a constant drip, drip, drip, that was reacting like
a refined form of torture upon her quivering nerves.

She made a supreme effort to widen her eyelids,
then focused hard upon Luiz's stiffly offended back
in an effort to stay awake, determined not to give
him the satisfaction of hearing her complain that she
was cold, wet, hungry, and almost delirious with
exhaustion.

Her one consolation was the conviction that they

had almost reached the river. Just audible in the
distance was the unmistakable sound of water crashing over rocks and boulders, an indication that they
were nearing the only rapids they had encountered
on their journey towards the village, less than a mile
from the spot on the river bank where the boat had
been left anchored.

Another hour must have passed before, in a voice
utterly devoid of compassion, Luiz indicated a fallen
tree trunk.

'Sit there while I rummage in the knapsacks to see
what I can find for breakfast.'

Hating his ease of movement, his incredible absence of fatigue, Rebel lowered herself stiffly on to
the log and stretched out her legs to ease the weight
from her pounding feet.

'A couple of biscuits each is all that can be spared,'
he frowned into the almost empty knapsack, 'unless
we manage to catch some fish or a paca or two we
must resign ourselves to going hungry for the next
couple of days.'

'What is paca?' she enquired, chewing miserably
upon a mouthful of damp biscuit with a predominant
flavour of mould.

'A very tasty rodent,' he sickened her, 'considered
by the Indians to be a great delicacy.'

Suspecting that his cruelty was intentional, she
controlled an impulse to vomit and strove to blank
off her disgust by deliberately changing the subject.
Small drifts of petals lay scattered at her feet, and as
she raised her eyes to the forest ceiling she saw others

wafting downward as a breeze rustled through the roof of thatched leaves.

'I've seen very few flowers in the forest,' she offered thoughtfully, 'and yet their strong, sweet perfume is all around us.'

'They bloom unseen up there in full daylight,' Luiz nodded upwards towards the crown of trees, 'a secret garden profuse with innumerable species of orchid known to the natives as "daughters of the air", the only female species capable of thriving without regular doses of male adulation,' he concluded dryly.

'Your ability to discriminate must be at fault if you label all women frivolous and flighty,' she flashed, needled by his contemptuous assessment of her sex.

She regretted her impulsive retort immediately she fell victim to a barrage of grey-eyed scorn. 'Are you daring to pretend that you are an exception to that rule?' She winced from a flint-sharp look that made her acutely conscious of every crease, stain, and rent in her disreputable outfit and felt humiliation, stinging as a slap, when he continued coldly, 'I have no doubt that even weeds nurture pretensions towards the appeal of orchids when I recall a certain young woman with a flower tucked behind each ear and a strategically-placed button left enticingly undone.'

Fiery-cheeked, she jumped to her feet to release a fraction of her humiliation in anger. 'You are despicable, *senhor*! As brutally insensitive as your slave-trading ancestors who curbed the spirits of men with the whip and inflicted even worse degradation upon their womenfolk. Saffira once said that you are married to the Amazon,' she choked, feeling once more stripped of modesty, 'which is just as it should be, for the Amazon possesses qualities that exactly match your own—a civilised outer shell hiding a savagely barbaric, cruelly insensitive interior.'

'So, I am the beast who threatens to ravage the gentle deer, eh?' he scathed in a drawl. 'Your talent for acting is considerable, *senhorita*, but you tax the credibilities of your audience with such swift changes of role. After all, most people—with the exception of novices such as Paulo—would consider your transition from huntress to distressed doe too incongruous to be believed!'

Although the timing was all wrong, his mood savagely suspicious, Rebel wanted desperately to clear up his misunderstanding about herself and Paulo, who stood like a ghostly barrier between them, whose supposed ill treatment formed the basis of every bitter confrontation, whose name was a spear Luiz used persistently to jab her conscience.

'I'm tired of being labelled a cheap, flirtatious hypocrite!' she flared, impatient of caution. 'You have entirely misread the situation between myself and Paulo. Even a criminal is allowed a hearing, but you've taken it upon yourself to act as judge and jury without even giving me a chance to explain.'

'To plead mitigating circumstances...?' His lip curled. 'Spare me the melodrama, *senhorita*, I can see that you are itching to play the role of injured innocent.'

'You're intolerant,' she accused steadily. 'You dislike me because you don't know me; you will never know me if you cling to your dislike of me.'

She knew her accusation of prejudice had struck at the heart of his conscience when he drew himself erect to defend, 'I act as a victim of experience. But speak your piece, if you must, I'll try hard not to dwell upon the fact that you are a chameleon whose colour adapts easily to prevailing circumstances.'

Heartened by her small victory, she felt confident enough to admit, 'From our first moment of meeting Paulo showed signs of being smitten, but I did nothing to encourage what was obviously a bad case of calf love. But neither did I discourage him, for to have done so would have been unkind to a boy who believed himself mature.'

'Mature enough to make love to you?' His question was dangerously casual.

'He kissed me—once,' she blustered, wondering what thoughts were sharpening his cloud-grey eyes.

'And you do not consider a kiss to be encouragement?' he persisted silkily.

Suddenly she felt herself floundering. 'Well, yes, perhaps ... but I was desperate, you see ... desperate for someone to guide me to the Indian village. I considered my father's reputation was at stake, his series of books had won world-wide acclaim and naturally he wanted his last volume to match the standard of its predecessors. I wanted it too, so much that I talked myself into believing that Paulo would be a competent guide—even refused to listen when at the last moment he lost his nerve and tried to back out. I was wrong to persuade him against his will,' she confessed, staring, unconsciously pleading, into hard eyes that showed no hint of softening, 'it was also wrong of me to encourage him to disobey your orders. For both of those errors I apologise, but I cannot and will not accept penance for sins I have not committed.'

'Are you asking me to believe that Paulo risked his reputation, his career, even his life, for the sake of one kiss?'

'Why not?' she asked him quietly, 'when everyone who knows him well remarks upon his kindness, his solicitude, and his abundance of chivalry.'

'Paulo may be possessed of many good qualities, but all of them are human,' he grated. 'You speak of him as a boy, then in the next breath you credit him with virtues that are supernatural. Make no mistake about it, *senhorita*, no man, whatever his age, can spend days in close proximity with a beautiful girl and expect to emerge with his emotions unscathed.'

Although his expression was bleak, his words bitten, a thrill of hope surged through her veins at this first faint hint that he found her attractive. She had suffered the wild, sweet agony of his kisses, had been shaken to the edge of sanity by the urgency of his caresses, yet always she had held back, confused and hurt by his lack of vocal commitment, by the absence of one small, vital word of love.

Newly-born hope was reflected in the tenderness of her eyes, in the curve of her tremulous mouth when she dared to continue pleading Paulo's cause.

'Please, Luiz,' his name sighed past her lips softly as a sob, 'don't lay the burden of my faults upon Paulo's shoulders! You know that the blame is entirely mine, so if you must punish someone let it be me.'

She was puzzled by the anger that forked, lightning-swift, through storm-grey eyes, an uncontrollable ire that seemed to erupt at every mention of Paulo's name.

'If he is ever to develop into a character strong enough to tame a rebel, he must learn to accept his punishment like a man,' he clipped ferociously. 'You have made plain your aversion to be *pawed*, but though a cub's playful strokes may tug at your maternal heartstrings, such emotion is no substitute for the passion that can only be aroused by a demanding mate!'

Rebel blushed fiercely at this callous reminder of episodes during which he had forced from her the unsheathed responses of a primitive she-cat, ripping the gauze from wounds so sensitive the exposure left her quivering. Her immediate instinct was to cower, but then pride came to her rescue, enabling her to deride the intolerance of a man permanently cursed by the devil riding on his shoulder.

'Are you so immune to folly, *senhor*, that you cannot forgive a young man one solitary lapse? Or is your unreasonable behaviour due to the fact that you find it harder to pardon a folly which you have committed yourself? If Paulo deserves to suffer the consequences of one kiss, then what punishment, might I ask, is applicable to you?'

The forest surroundings seemed to fall into a hush as they glared at each other, oblivious to fatigue, to the need for haste, to approaching danger, to everything except their mutual contempt. It took the screech of a startled bird to alert Luiz to danger. His black head jerked into a listening attitude before tersely he swung round to her.

'Make towards the river, *quickly*!' he urged, bending to retrieve the knapsacks. 'Unless I've misjudged, we should find the motor launch anchored just a few hundred yards from here.'

Whichever sound his keen ears had recognised lent an urgency to his stride that she found impossible to match, but immediately she showed signs of lagging his hand shot out to grip her elbow, propelling her so roughly she almost fell headlong into the under-brush. Sensing that his action was motivated by need rather than by malice, she submitted without protest to being half dragged, half hoisted towards the river with a speed that barely left her feet time to make contact with the ground.

The lagoon when they reached it was as becalmed and debris-strewn as when he had left it. Wasting no time on words, Luiz flung the knapsacks to the ground and with unerring judgment pounced upon the boat left so well camouflaged Rebel had imagined it would take ages to find.

Made panicky by his obvious presentiment of danger, she joined him in tossing aside the leaves and ferns cocooning the boat and was glad to obey his terse instruction to scramble aboard. The sound of the motor was music to her ears, sweet notes suddenly soured by inhuman yells accompanying a burst of black bodies on to the river bank.

From halfway across the lagoon it was impossible to tell whether the howling natives were registering anger or despair, whether their gesticulating arms implied threat or were merely waving a fond farewell. A glance at Luiz' profile, set hard with regret, confirmed that he, too, was uncertain and at the same time gained her swift insight to his feelings. For years he had devoted all his interest to the welfare of the forgotten tribes, courageously penetrating their territory alone and unarmed in an attempt to cultivate their trust and affection. But now, owing to her blundering interference, everything he had worked for seemed to hang in the balance. Did they still regard him as a friend whose visits were cherished? Or was he now an object of hatred, the man who had robbed them of their goddess?

Impelled by the certainty that in spite of the danger involved he would return to find out, she rose to her feet and stood facing the natives with her arms open wide, mutely pleading his cause.

'*Meu Deus! Sit down!*' Luiz yelled across his shoulder as he manipulated the controls. 'We are still within range of their blowpipes!'

Terrified by the threat, but determined not to give ground, she began waving farewell, aching for a friendly response. The natives' bodies had been re-

duced to mere spots upon the shore when across the
lagoon floated the sound of chanting. When swiftly
Luiz killed the motor, straining his ears to listen, her
legs collapsed beneath her, so that she was deposited
in a limp heap at the bottom of the boat.

'What are they saying?' she begged, scanning his
unreadable profile.

His concentration was so intense he seemed not to
have heard, but then as if the heat of her stare had
penetrated a mask of ice, his gravity dissolved into a
slowly-warming smile. Even then he seemed in no
hurry to put her out of her suspense, the lazy slap of
water against the sides of the boat; the natives' chanting fading into the distance, the fierce rays of sun
tinting his profile golden as the mask of an Inca god,
all had time to become imprinted upon her memory
before his pride-ridden mouth managed to form the
admission:

'You are a very courageous young lady, Senhorita
Storm. To have shown fear while still within range of
their weapons would have been human, but because
you displayed the composure expected of an
Amazon, they are now chanting a plea that their
goddess might soon return.'

'Oh...!' Her mouth retained its circle of surprise
while she savoured the effect of his rare compliment.
For once, she had managed to find favour! Relief,
heady as a draught of champagne, swept sparkles
into her wide blue eyes.

As if he, too, was struggling with unfamiliar emotions, Luiz turned away to switch on the engine, then focused his attention upon guiding the boat through the narrow exit from the lagoon before nosing into the confusing maze of waterways.

After an hour of silent travelling through a world of water and forest, he unbent far enough to throw the odd enlightening remark across his shoulder, reading in her absorption a deep fascination with the pressing forest that seemed to have remained unchanged since prehistoric times, whose roots drove deep into the primeval past.

Gauging her thoughts with uncanny accuracy, he reminded her lightly, 'If you are comparing the Amazon with other equatorial forests you might have encountered in Africa or the Far East, you must bear in mind the fact that this area has remained undisturbed for millions of years and that as a consequence plants and animals have been able to evolve without interference, taking on unrecognisable shapes and forms, resulting in a greater variety of unknown animal and plant species than any other place on earth.'

'I'm wishing I hadn't used up all my film,' Rebel confessed, anxious to prolong the conversation with the stranger whose indefinable change of attitude had rendered her strangely shy.

'Is there any particular omission that you wish to rectify?' he enquired so casually he did not bother even to turn his head.

'I should have liked to concentrate upon theatrical

effects to stimulate the imagination—such things as raindrops glistening upon a lotus-leaf platter,' she waved a vague hand in the air, 'a mass of caterpillars flung like a crocheted pink and white shawl across a fallen tree trunk; ribbed sandbanks that look splotched on to canvas by the brush of an eccentric artist. But most of all,' she decided thoughtfully, 'I should have liked to have been able to photograph some of the species of orchid that flower high on the roof of the forest, the ones you say the natives call "daughters of the air".'

She wondered what had motivated his sudden impulse to steer the boat to the river bank and then, with his rifle slung across one shoulder, to step ashore with the whimsical instruction:

'Stay there, I won't be long.'

Mutely she watched him stride off into the forest, then seconds later jerked with fright when the crack of a rifle set wings fluttering and angry bird calls screeching through the forest.

Her shock was intensified when he returned to drop a flower in her lap, a blossom he had plucked with a bullet from its aerial garden, its perfume heady as narcotic, its passion-red flowers clinging velvet-soft to her cupped fingers.

'How lovely ...' she breathed, moved almost to tears by his apparent thoughtfulness, then recognised his gift as a peace-offering when he leant his dark head close to astound her by saying:

'Any flower can excite praise in an exotic setting, but my own admiration is reserved for the pert and pretty flowers mistakenly classed as weeds that achieve full and gorgeous bloom even in the face of adversity.'

CHAPTER THIRTEEN

THE moment the sun went down troupes of monkeys had begun chattering in the trees and myriad tune-less bird noises—whistles, creaks, screeches—had combined with the croaking of frogs and the hiss and gurgle of the river into a background of noise far from conducive to sleep.

Luiz had lighted two fires, one close to Rebel's hammock and the other just a yard or so away next to his own. But as Rebel lay wide awake staring at palm trees silhouetted by the moon into a line of slender ghosts with heads rearing into an indigo sky slashed with lightning, she shivered and curled up into a ball in an effort to combat the chill of damp night air that was penetrating her sleeping bag. She felt exhausted, yet her mind was far too active to allow her to sleep.

Since the incident when he had presented her with the orchid, Luiz had become strangely reticent. For hour after silent hour, he had guided the launch along the 'narrows', countless miles of waterways, sometimes narrow enough for foliage on opposite banks to meet overhead, at other times widening into lakes so immense their shoreline was a faint blur on the horizon.

Rebel's attention swung towards Luiz who, since she had retired, had remained sitting next to the campfire gazing into flames that reflected tiny, dancing devils in his eyes and cast a mask of gold over his brooding features. Made peevish by the cold, and by her inability to fathom a mood he had drawn around him like a cloak he seemed in no hurry to discard, she changed position and began wriggling her toes in an effort to stave off the clutch of cramp from numbed feet. The creak of her hammock attracted his attention. She saw him rise to his feet, then tensed when he began making his way towards her.

'Can't you sleep?' His tone was as coolly detached as his looming shadow, completely enveloping, yet totally lacking in substance.

'I'm afraid not,' she replied through chattering teeth, then gasped when a shiver raked icy fingers down her spine.

He hesitated, and though his expression was shadowed she sensed his frown, heard a note of reluctance in his voice when finally he offered:

'Would you like to join me in a swim?'

'A swim...?' She shot upright with surprise. 'But it's far too cold—and dangerous!'

'It is customary for the natives to bathe at this time of night, for when the temperature in the forest is at its lowest the water is considerably more com-

fortable than the damp chill of the night air. Also,'
he explained, 'when we were setting up camp I discovered a forest stream that is completely uncon-
taminated, water pure enough to drink.'

'Well ... if you're sure.' Rebel clenched her teeth
to still their chattering as he helped her out of the
hammock. 'Anything will be better than lying here
freezing.'

Immediately he set her on her feet Luiz withdrew
his support with a haste that underlined his reluctance to make physical contact, an action so far removed from his previous conduct her temperature
rose at the snub. She stumbled in his wake through
the forest, fighting waves of hurt and confusion
caused by his changed attitude. Earlier that day she
had imagined their relationship had taken a turn for
the better, but for some reason he had withdrawn
into a shell of politeness that was a marked contrast
to the heated exchanges she now realised she had
enjoyed—almost as much as the angry embraces and
fiery kisses whose absence left her feeling deprived.

This time she was given no cause to feel embarrassed by his presence when she shivered out of her
clothes and dipped a tentative toe into the shallows
of a pool formed by a drop in the bed of a gently
coursing stream. There was no sign of Luiz when she
braced and then dived into depths so agonisingly
cold that she shot to the surface spluttering and gasp-
ing to replace the breath that had been shocked from
her lungs. But surprisingly, as she trod water in an
effort to regain her composure before swimming

towards the bank, she felt a tingling of warmth
spreading through her limbs, then gradually as she
took time to assimilate the startling beauty of the
moon-bathed pool, scintillating red as a ruby bathed
in moonbeams, she felt the warmth of the water in-
crease until she was enjoying the pleasurable sensation of swimming naked in a vat of warm red wine.

She cavorted with sinful enjoyment, lost in a fanciful dream that excluded the mundane fact that the
colour of the water owed its origin to a geographical
pattern that could have been simply explained by
any amateur geologist. Her rapture was so complete
that when Luiz's head rose out of the wine-dark
water she blinked, then murmured dreamily:

'Bacchus, god of pleasure, clothed for peace in a
robe of purple, and for war in a panther's skin!'

For a second he looked blank, then when realisation dawned he tossed a mane of damp hair out of
his eyes and countered dryly:

'Bacchus was credited with the wearing of many
different cloaks, among them that of the evil demon,
and also the lord of destiny. I will not embarrass you
by asking which of those two you consider suits me
best.' Giving her no time to indicate her choice, he
turned to cleave through the water, calling across his
shoulder, 'It is time to dry out, young bacchante, you
have imbibed long enough!'

Reluctantly, Rebel followed his example, but
when she reached the bank and stepped out of the
pool she felt she had stepped straight into an icy
grip that pinched her veins until her blood froze.

Belatedly rueing the absence of a towel, she struggled to ease her clothes over her dripping body, then tried to cancel out her folly by weakly massaging her limbs.

'Are you ready?' Luiz stepped from behind a screen of trees, but at the sight of a face pinched with cold, at a shirt plastered with strands of dripping hair, he choked back a curse and replaced it with a snap of impatience that could have had its roots in the sight of her distress or in his own anger at being blind to the obvious. Whichever it was, he wasted no time on words but whipped off his shirt and used it to smother her protest while he rubbed her hair dry, not stopping until her scalp was tingling, her hair fluffed into a golden cloud.

Still intensely aggravated, he then swept her up into his arms and strode with her back to the camp, where he deposited her with a jolt next to the camp-fire whose flames still crackled a welcoming ring of warmth.

Gratefully, Rebel sank to her knees and crouched nearer with her arms outstretched to thaw her chilled fingers. Her body felt weak with the combined effects of cold and Luiz's rough treatment, which was probably why she reacted with uncontrollable trembling to his harsh condemnation.

'It is times such as this that prove beyond doubt that women are unsuited to the rigours involved in travelling unexplored territory! Why can't females be satisfied with doing what they do best—namely, keeping house and bringing up children?'

She had no idea what had made him so angry, and still less idea why she was having to fight an urge to cry.

'That is a question I often asked myself,' she choked, 'especially whenever I feel the child inside me crying out for the dolls she never had, for the playmates she never knew.'

To her horror tears began spilling down her cheeks, so huge, fast, and furious they rained down upon the fire and were sizzled into extinction. She heard a muttered imprecation high above her head, then was drawn to her feet by a grip she expected to be rough but which she found surprisingly gentle.

'You are tired and you are cold,' flatly Luiz addressed her downbent head, 'too cold to be left to sleep alone. If you remember, *senhorita*, I did warn you that there would be nights in the Amazon when you would have to be prepared to share your companions' body heat—it would seem,' he concluded grimly, 'that this is one of those nights.'

He showed no sign of emotion as he spread his sleeping bag next to the fire and helped her into it, but it would not have mattered to her if he had, for she was too cold and dispirited to care. Not even when he slid alongside her did she flinch from the intimacy of a body resting rigid as a tree trunk against her back.

Only one disturbing thought moved her to murmur:

'Will we be safe from prowlers, do you think, flat on the forest floor?'

'Don't worry, I'll keep my rifle close to hand.'

'Yes, but . . .' She began a protest, then had to stop to smother a yawn.

'You will be perfectly safe, *senhorita*,' he insisted, then, displaying once again an uncanny ability to read her thoughts, he concluded with bleak irony, 'I can safely promise that I will not fall asleep.'

She stirred restlessly during the night, wakening with his name on her lips, then sinking back immediately into a warm, contented abyss, reassured by the sound of his steady breathing and by the nearness of a body, still and unyielding as one of the fallen tree trunks that supplied protection to defenceless creatures of the forest, to butterflies that crowded their hollows, and to fragile flowers that emerged, stemless, from their bark, then remained clinging— tenaciously as only the delicate can cling—during the whole of their brief lifetime.

When fingers of dawn light prodded her awake she stirred, then frowned, sensing a lack of warmth, the absence of a heartbeat, powerful as a dynamo, that had throbbed new life into her frozen body.

'Good morning, *senhorita*.' Luiz's tone was cool enough to make her wonder if she had spent the whole night dreaming, or if he really had shared her bed.

'Good morning.' She sat up, flustered, to eye his tanned face and the tangle of damp hair that told her he was freshly bathed.

'I've managed to find some bananas for breakfast,' he continued, mundanely as if he had just popped

down to some nearby market place. 'The biscuits are
finished, and there is only water left to drink—but
in that respect, at least, we are lucky, for in some
parts of the forest the water is unsuitable for drinking.'

'Then shouldn't we fill the containers before we
go?' Rebel queried, disconcerted by his air of detachment.

'Unfortunately, in our haste to leave the village the
containers were left behind,' he told her, uncensori-
ous but dry. 'However, at this time of the year there
is a short cut through the waterways that becomes
navigable, so if we set off without delay we might
just avoid the discomfort of spending another night
in the forest.'

He had said discomfort, but what he had really
meant was disaster, she decided, as she watched him
concentrate the whole of his attention upon navigat-
ing twists and turns, bends, then straight stretches of
river along which he sent the launch hurtling at
demoniacal speed, using intense concentration and
physical effort as a vent for some inner frustration.

As the launch skimmed across the water, stirring
anacondas from the beds of dark, swampy pools,
agitating alligators heaped like harmless logs upon
sunny sandbanks, startling screeches and an angry
flapping of wings from flocks of unsuspecting water
birds, Rebel felt a need to apologise to the indignant
forest dwellers whose peace was being shattered by
the intrusion of an impatiently speeding demon.

They stopped only once, to explore the forest for

food and drink, only to discover, as the Indians had many years before, that parts of the luxuriant Amazon were as barren as a desert. Rebel was scrambling along the edge of the river bank, her eyes searching hungrily for signs of fruit, when she tripped over a root and instinctively flung out her hands to cushion her fall. The pain of red-hot needles jabbed her palms when she made contact with a nearby tree, its trunk banded from top to bottom with sharp spines. Uttering a cry of pain, she pulled them away, then stared wide-eyed at bristles stuck numerous as pins into the fleshy cushions of her palms.

Predictably, Luiz, who always made certain that she remained within earshot, was drawn by her cry and erupted beside her in a matter of seconds.

'What's wrong...?' His keen eyes scoured the underbrush for snakes, then, satisfied that there were none, he rustled through bushes that might have been housing some predator. Suspecting that since early morning he had been seeking an excuse to be angry with her, Rebel jerked her hands behind her back and had the grace to colour slightly when she lied:

'I'm sorry if my cry sounded urgent, I was startled by a bird that flew out of a bush.'

Her blush deepened when, instead of seeming satisfied, he began studying her face as if weighing up whether her expression was betraying apology or guilt. Made uncomfortable by the intensity of his stare, she sought escape by moving aside, wondering fretfully why a man who had not hesitated to believe her implications that she made a habit of cultivating the opposite sex should be so hard to deceive in other respects.

'Wait...!' When his detaining hand jolted her arm he immediately noticed her wince. Without a word, he manacled her wrist with steely fingers and drew her hand upwards, turning it over to expose the palm. His hiss was so aggravated she tensed, then waited miserably for a verbal axe to fall.

But he sounded surprisingly civilised, pleasantly conversational, in fact, when after he had weathered the intial shock of examining her bristling palms, he told her levelly, 'There is a medicine chest in the launch, we had better make our way there.'

His tone had sounded so devoid of expression she felt slighted. Was he disinterested, had he mentally labelled her a peril-prone nuisance? Or could his calmness be compared with the prelude to an Amazon storm, a time of heavy oppression, harnessed elements, a dangerous build-up of passion that could only find release in fiery wrath?

In spite of his wish to reach home before nightfall, he sat for best part of an hour tweezing the bristles out of her swollen palms. Then he rubbed ointment into the wounds and applied bandages with the quick, neat skill of a professional.

'Now,' he steamed quietly as a simmering kettle, 'will you please remain in the launch while I fetch us something to eat and drink?'

Rebel watched perplexed as he swung himself over the side of the launch and strode without a backward look into the belt of trees. She did as he had instructed, sensing waves emanating from his direction, daring her to follow. Even when macaws screamed raucous insults as they wheeled overhead and a black bird, huge as a pheasant, left its perch on a rock in the middle of the river and fanned her with its draught as it flew past her into the forest, she remained still and deep in troubled thought.

No more than ten minutes had passed when he returned carrying a couple of lengths of hacked-off liana, balancing them carefully so that the ends were not allowed to droop, he handed her one, then demonstrated their purpose by placing one end of the piece he had retained to his lips and tipping the other end upright.

She hesitated to follow his example, wondering what sort of taste to expect, but once his thirst had been quenched he assured her, 'It is quite tasteless, pure drinking water. Were it not for this particular species of water-holding liana many natives would die of thirst in this region where there are no forest streams, especially during the drier months when they are unable to collect rainwater.'

Encouraged, Rebel lifted the liana tube to her lips and tipped the end until a flow of water cooled her tongue. The piece of liana, over a foot long, which Luiz had severed with a machete, held sufficient liquid to allow her to drink her fill, and that, together with the avocado pears he had stuffed into his pockets, formed the basis of a tasteless yet filling meal.

Even before he had finished eating he started up
the motor and a short while later the launch erupted
out of a narrow waterway into a huge lake, its surface rippled by breeze, where freshwater dolphins
were sporting among the waves as if putting on a
show of aquatic skill for the benefit of fishing birds
circling overhead.

Rebel became so entranced by their antics she just
had to leave her seat to join him at the wheel.

'There's so many of them,' she gasped.

'That is because their numbers are protected by
myth,' he yelled above the roar of the engine. 'Although dolphin flesh is edible, the natives won't eat
it because they believe it will make them impotent.'

For a while he allowed her to remain beside him,
enjoying the rush of breeze through her hair, the
tingle of spray against her cheeks, then made her
feel an intruder by curtly dismissing her.

'Better get back to your seat.' He reduced the
speed of the launch, frowning at great rafts of greenery floating towards them. As he inched the launch
forward she saw that they were masses of floating
plant cover that seemed solid enough to bear her
weight. His tension was communicated to her as he
manoeuvred a careful passage through matted water
grass that closed in their wake, making the launch
seem landlocked, not so much sailing as ploughing a
furrow.

Intensely attuned to his mood, she sensed relief
relaxing the curve of his taut shoulders as the matted
grass became sparser and sparser, until finally they

left behind them the rolling meadow of vegetation
he had obviously feared might hold them fast,
marooned as if shipwrecked on an uncharted island.

Many silent hours later it became evident from the
sure way Luiz was steering the launch that, though
night had fallen, he was able to recognise familiar
landmarks, that waterways which to her seemed
monotonously identical held a message that told him
they were nearly home.

With a mixture of joy and sorrow she saw a land-
ing stage loom out of the darkness, heard the engine
noise fade, felt a bump when the launch collided
gently with wooden stakes driven deep into the river
bed, and knew that her father, Paulo, Saffira de Pas
and a host of other intruders were mere minutes
away.

At if he, too, felt they had reached the end of a
chapter, some parts of which he was wishing could
have been re-written, Luiz did not immediately jump
ashore but sat down opposite, his face an indistinct
blur in the darkness.

'We have arrived,' he told her with rough-edge
finality.

'I'm sure you're not sorry,' she whispered, close to
tears, 'they say that the Amazon is a woman—more
woman than any one man can handle—yet you've
had her to cope with as well as myself.'

'I have reached the conclusion, *senhorita*,' he replied harshly, 'that the Amazon and yourself are
indivisible, identical twins who share the same characteristics, the same contradictions, the same ability

to attract and repel. To the passing traveller you can be both cruel and kind, encouraging a man's confidence so that he strides without fear along familiar paths, only to topple without warning into a pit of doubt. Your thoughts, like the Amazon's maze of waterways, are devious; your actions as unpredictable as her rapids. Yes, the Amazon is most certainly female,' he concluded heavily, 'the only woman I've ever willingly shared—the only one for whom I am prepared to be listed "one of many lovers".'

CHAPTER FOURTEEN

REBEL craned her neck to study lines of newly-developed prints pegged up to dry. For the past days the darkroom that Luiz's scientists had willingly improvised had been used as a retreat, a place where she could escape from countless questions, curious looks, and the occasional jocular innuendo. But most of all its construction had helped to make work a valid excuse for avoiding Luiz Manchete, the man who, from the moment he had crossed his own threshold, had resumed the role of Senhor—an aloof figure of authority whose cool air of detachment discouraged flippant questions, one whom everyone—with the exception of Saffira—held very much in awe.

Were it not that she had photographs as evidence, she might have been tempted to believe that the events they had shared were figments of her imagination, but as it was, each scene that emerged from its bath of developing fluid revived vivid memories of days filled with wonder, with strife, with danger and with occasional almost unbearable happiness.

Unfortunately, her work was now finished. As she hung up the last print to dry she stared with dawning excitement at the face of the headman, contorted with fury, at his crudely fashioned wig and the host of female fripperies that clashed incongruously against his wiry warrior frame. Her breath caught in a gulp as she examined the print and caught for the first time the full impact of the headman's fury—the upraised spear, the black hand clenching a blowpipe! Had she really risked the consequences of such primitive fury? No wonder Luiz had ranted about her stupidity! It hurt to know that he held her in such low esteem; especially when she had to acknowledge that she had only herself to blame.

'Rebel...!' Paulo rapped on the door as he called out her name. 'Can I come in?'

'Wait just a second!' she stammered, jolted back to earth, then began a panic-stricken rush to hide a pile of prints whose subject was too personal to share. Pushing them inside an unsealed envelope, she utilised a shelf full of books as a temporary hideout before assuring Paulo:

'All right, it's safe now to come in!'

As he stepped inside the darkroom, no larger than a cubbyhole, Rebel could tell immediately that he was excited. For days he had lived with the shadow of reprimand hanging over him, the threat of being dismissed from the job he loved and the consequent risk to his career. With typical cruelty, Luiz had kept him in suspense; since his arrival home he had spent most of each day inside his study dealing with correspondence that had accumulated during his absence, yet Rebel felt certain that if he had wanted to he could have placed Paulo's interview at the top of his agenda.

'I've just been speaking with the Senhor,' he blurted, almost beside himself with excitement.

She smiled her relief and in spite of the fact that the outcome had obviously been favourable, felt compelled to ask:

'How did you get on?'

Perching on the edge of a table, he expelled a sigh that was a mixture of wonder and slight disbelief, then began recounting slowly, as if the sound of his own voice helped rid him of doubt.

'Very well, I found him surprisingly sympathetic. After a grim preliminary lecture on the folly of disobeying orders, he changed his attitude completely and began talking to me like a Dutch uncle, touching lightly upon the influence an experienced woman can wield over a youth such as myself; confiding that even older, more worldly men could fall victim to the wiles of designing females.'

Rebel choked back a gasp of hurt, knowing full well that it was herself he had been referring to, and appalled by her own stupidity in projecting an image far removed from the person she actually was.

That Paulo had also recognised her as the villainess of the piece was obvious when he grinned: 'In the past, I have always admired the Senhor's ability to assess and judge correctly, but in this instance,' he assured her sweetly troubled face, 'his judgment has gone completely haywire. And I told him so!' He stood upright, posturing proudly. 'I made it plain to him that even at the risk of jeopardising my career, I could not listen without protest to erroneous remarks being made about the girl I intended to marry!'

Rebel's mind was so busy grappling with the knowledge that she ranked even lower than she had imagined in Luiz's estimation, that for a second his statement did not register. It was not until he grabbed her close to snatch an eager, clumsy kiss that she realised the sense of his words.

'No, Paulo, you mustn't...!' Jerking her mouth from his, she thrust him at arm's length. 'How could you say such a thing, I've never given you the slightest reason to suppose ...' she choked, then trembled into appalled silence, wondering what Luiz Manchete would be thinking of her now, how much his attitude would be hardened by the misconception that she had picked up her flirtation with Paulo where she had supposedly left off.

Yet she had to feel sympathy for the boy whose expression was a reflection of how she was feeling—hurt and miserably dejected.

'I thought . . .' he began, then hesitated. 'I've made a mess of proposing, haven't I?' he accepted sadly. 'While you were away in the jungle I was so frantically worried about you, you filled my thoughts every minute of every day, so much so that it seemed a logical conclusion that a girl who had come to mean so much to me should eventually become my wife. I love you, Rebel,' he pleaded miserably. 'It simply never occurred to me that you might not love me in return.'

A few painful minutes later she made her way to her bedroom, slightly heartened by the knowledge that Paulo, though upset, had accepted his rejection without malice.

When she stepped over the threshold she frowned, her search for solitude thwarted by her father's presence in her room.

'Rebel, my dear,' he beamed, then nodded towards a large cardboard box placed on top of her bed, 'I've brought you a present—and some good news.'

'Thank you, Father.' She made an effort to sound grateful, but merely managed to achieve a tone of listless surprise. 'As there's been a dearth of good news lately, I'll hear that first and open my present later.'

'How can you say such a thing!' His eyebrows rose. 'You arrived back from your expedition safe and well with superlative prints, better than I could ever have hoped for, yet still you're not satisfied. What further ambition are you hoping to achieve?'

She was tempted to tell him the truth, to tell him that the challenge of exploring unknown places had lost all appeal, that the thought of spending the rest of her life wandering like a vagrant with no fixed abode, never staying in one place long enough to put down roots, was a prospect so appalling that just to think of it made her feel ill. The only other alternative—that of settling down in some country cottage to keep her father company during his retirement—held a lack of stimulation she found depressing. But he was so happy, so delighted at the prospect of beginning on his final book, she simply could not upset him.

'As Senhor Manchete once implied, I'm an ungrateful wretch,' she concluded solemnly.

'Not at all,' he contradicted. 'You're feeling a little flat, that's all—quite a natural reaction after an exciting expedition. Fortunately, I have just the tonic you need.' He slipped a hand inside his pocket and withdrew a sheet of newspaper, pointing to a paragraph he had outlined in pencil. 'Remember the photographs you took of Mount Kinabalu when we were working in Borneo last year? Well, one of them, a dramatic shot of a cloud-filled gully, has won the "Most Outstanding Picture of the Year" award!'

'Really...!' Rebel wished she could share his proud enthusiasm.

Seemingly unaware of her disinterest, he continued, 'We wouldn't have known about it if I hadn't asked Paulo to fetch back any English newspapers he could lay his hands on when, quite unexpectedly, he was forced to fly to the capital on business. I could hardly believe my eyes when I read the paragraph, so brief it almost escaped my notice. It made me so proud, and so thankful I'd had the foresight to ask Paulo to purchase your present even before I became aware of your success. It's a dress,' he confided, indicating once more the cardboard box on her bed. 'You've never shown much interest in your appearance, my dear, probably because you were deprived of feminine influence at a very early age, but basically you must be as keen on dressing up as other girls of your age. It will please me very much to see you looking as pretty as you're able, so wear the dress this evening for what will have to be our farewell dinner if we're to reach London in time for the presentation of the award.'

Rebel did not bother to unpack the dress until long after he had gone, but sat for hours stunned by the thought that the gulf between herself and Luiz Manchete was to be stretched by miles of jungle and sea, that dinner this evening would be the last meal they would share, that when she retired that night it would be to sleep for the very last time beneath his roof.

Without her becoming aware of it, the room became filled with nocturnal shadows. She was jerked back to reality by the screech of a monkey calling its mate, a sound projecting all the proud arrogance, the naked need to mate that she was always to associate with the jungle.

Luiz preferred to dine late, so she had ample time to shampoo and dry her hair before binding it into heavy golden coils that left her slender neck exposed, a slim stem drooping beneath a weight of care.

Displaying unerring good taste and a deep devotion to his subject, Paulo had chosen for her an ankle-length dress in a soft shade of mauve that cast a veil of mystery over eyes doused with sadness and stroked pastel shadows under high cheekbones and inside vulnerable hollows left bare by a low scooped neckline. The skirt flowed in fine pleats to settle just above her ankles, whispering soft, silken sighs at the least hint of movement.

She stared into a mirror, slightly shy of voluptuous curves usually kept camouflaged by a uniform of drill shirt and trousers; heartened by a hand-span waist much more slender than Saffira de Pas's; bemused by the romantic aura of sleeves that billowed, then belled out over tight wristbands. Paulo had even had the foresight to provide matching footwear, high-heeled sandals that cobwebbed her feet and clasped fine-boned ankles within strips of pastel blue leather.

Fired by an impulse to be daring, by an urge to make Luiz Manchete aware that some men might consider her desirable even *outside* the jungle, she searched her bag for an almost forgotten present, a small box containing a palette of eyeshadow and a lipstick that had lain unopened and unused since the day she had received it.

Her fingers quivered as nervously she stroked soft blue shadow on to her lids. Then carefully, but with increased confidence, she outlined a curving upper lip and concluded her artistry by painting in a colourful pink pout.

She put down the lipstick to examine the results of her handiwork, staring intently at the sophisticated stranger whose image she saw reflected in the mirror. She had seen similar images in the pages of glossy magazines, had often envied them their look of fragility and the cosseted, pampered life style that seemed an essential equivalent to girls whose hair was never allowed to come into contact with brambles, whose complexions were protected from sun and wind, whose hands did not seem capable of sustaining the weight of a flower, much less a knapsack, camera, and heavy items of photographic equipment.

She tilted her head sideways to peer at one cheek marred by barely discernible scratches criss-crossing her skin, and sighed. It would have been nice if Luiz's last memory of her could have been one of perfection. With a helpless shrug she rose to her feet, trying to console herself with the thought that perfection could be slightly dull.

She left her room to make her way in the direction of a small *sala* where guests habitually gathered for pre-dinner drinks. Usually there was a crowd of scientists in which she could become lost, but when she stepped inside the room seemed empty. She hesitated, wondering if perhaps she was too early, or if drinks were being served in a different room. She was just about to turn on her heel when her ears caught the hiss of a sharply-indrawn breath. Her head spun in the direction of the sound and with a startled leap of her pulses she recognised Luiz, unfamiliarly elegant in a dinner jacket whose matt whiteness acted as a perfect foil for teak-chipped features and well disciplined, devil-black hair.

For a startled second they stared at each other, tense and wary as jungle cats in sudden confrontation, undecided whether to purr or claw. Then as Luiz remembered his duty as host, his glinting eyes became hooded as he offered with suave urbanity:

'Can I get you a drink?'

She blinked when a shaft of light fired brilliance into diamond-studded cuffs as he lifted a decanter filled with amber spirit.

'A fruit juice will do fine, thank you,' she stammered, feeling a threat even greater than the headman's spear. He prowled across the floor as if caged and handed her a glass filled almost to the brim, its surface bobbing with miniature ice-floes that clinked against the rim and frosted her tongue when she took her first sip.

'You are looking very lovely this evening.'

The compliment was so unexpected she spluttered and almost choked.

'You must not spoil your dress.' His face was expressionless as he mopped surplus fruit juice from the stem of her glass with a pristine handkerchief. 'Saffira tells me that Paulo expended a great deal of time and effort upon its purchase. Which is just as it should be, considering the importance of the occasion. I believe, *senhorita*, that congratulations are in order?' His voice clinked cold as the ice cubes in her glass as he prompted a response when she was slow to answer.

Realising that her father must have told him about the award, she felt her cheeks become suffused by an embarrassed blush.

'Yes, that's correct,' she jerked, completely at a loss for further words.

She recoiled from the heat of spears that flamed in his eyes, then became smothered by a curtain of bleak grey. Miserably she stared into her glass, wondering why he should be so aggravated by her success, and was rendered further confused when anger spilled into his words.

'Such a change of circumstances is bound to interfere with your work. I had the impression that you were a dedicated traveller, but surely, having accepted new responsibilities, you will be forced to settle down?'

For a moment she was puzzled, then vaguely she recalled her father rambling on about one of the benefits attached to the award—a chance for up-and-coming young photographers to work for one year with an expert in their own particular field.

'I may feel tied at first,' she stammered, 'but I'll keep in mind the fact that my freedom will not be restricted for ever. After a short time, I'll be able to carry on as before, but with much better prospects.'

Luiz's head jerked backwards and for a terrifying second she was reminded of an enraged cobra poised to strike. Then bringing tremendous effort to bear, he managed to contain his venom long enough to ice:

'Indeed you will, Senhorita Storm. You have done your homework well—one day Paulo will be a very wealthy young man!'

Ten solitary minutes later Rebel took her place at the dinner table, her stunned mind still struggling to assimilate the fact that she and Luiz had been talking at cross-purposes, that while she had imagined they were discussing her award he had, in actual fact, been referring to her non-existent engagement to Paulo.

In a horrified daze, she endured the discipline of having to pretend to eat each course that was placed in front of her, to somehow manage monosyllabic replies to remarks directed by Paulo and Saffira who, together with herself and her father, were the only guests at dinner that evening. But behind her screen of politeness she was frantically resurrecting every word they had exchanged, understanding why his every nuance of expression had betrayed amazement and utter contempt during the brief, disastrous interlude.

'Your daughter does not have much to say for herself this evening, Professor!' Saffira's complacently feline voice scratched Rebel's absorption.

'She is not a talkative child,' her father agreed. 'If only a camera could be employed as a medium of speech you would find her a brilliant conversationalist.'

'You must also make allowances for the fact that the *senhorita* has a great deal on her mind.' Luiz's voice sliced down from the head of the table. 'Many torments scatter the path towards matrimony.'

Every breath caught in surprise, then silence was broken simultaneously by both Paulo and her father.

'Forgive my omission, *senhor*,' Paulo uttered hastily, 'I have not yet had the opportunity——'

'The path towards matrimony...!' Her father interrupted, startled enough to forget his manners. 'My friend, that is one path I would dearly love to see my daughter tread, but as yet,' he sighed, 'there are no signs to indicate that such a happy prospect is within sight.'

Rebel wanted to run out of the room, terribly conscious of Luiz's white-knuckled fist grasped around the handle of his knife, of the rapt attention he paid to her father's words when sadly he continued, 'For that, I feel partly to blame. Because of my own self-interest, my absorption with my work, Rebel has spent her entire lifetime in the company of men, consequently she has been more closely protected than a cloistered nun.'

In response to Saffira's derisive laughter, he sent her an understanding smile. 'That must seem to you a contradiction of terms, *senhora*, but I'm certain Luiz will understand perfectly,' he glanced towards Luiz, whose sharpened features looked chipped by an axe, 'and will not contradict my theory when I remind him that seasoned explorers, men who live close to nature, will add miles to their journey rather than disturb a brood of chicks, will linger for hours admiring the beauty of unusual orchids, yet become enraged if one of their number, without very good reason, should as much as tamper with a stem. Am I not right, Luiz?' his challenge rang the length of the table. 'Have you ever known an instance when a woman's safety has been threatened or her trust abused, even when travelling in the company of one man?'

Rebel had never imagined herself feeling pity for the arrogant Portuguese, but when she saw him whiten, saw his fist tighten around the handle of his knife as if he would snap it in two, she knew that he was being tortured by the reminder of incidents that had assumed in his mind an aspect of barbarity, that he was comparing his actions with those of jungle beasts who seized every opportunity to mate, regardless of whether their victims were willing or unwilling.

She wanted to cry out an assurance that it did not matter, that everything he had done was cancelled out by his white, stricken look that emblazoned a message of guilt readable by even the least perceptive. But to her relief, neither her father nor Paulo seemed sufficiently intuitive.

But the same could not be said of Saffira, whose dark eyes sharpened to points as she delved Luiz's mind, deciphering not only his thoughts but the secret spaces between the lines.

She swung a glare of pure hatred in Rebel's direction and at the sight of a sweep of tell-tale colour she jumped to her feet to level the caustic accusation:

'You men are all so gullible, you see innocence where a woman sees only guilt, remain blind to truth that is staring you in the face!' Her chair crashed to the floor as she kicked it aside, then dashed as if demented out of the room. They were given no time to recover from their astonishment before she returned carrying a large envelope which Rebel immediately recognised.

Guessing Saffira's intention, she struggled to voice a protest, but could only manage to project a gasp from a throat that felt gripped by claws.

'If your innocent daughter is so fluent with her camera, Professor,' she triumphed, spilling a pile of photographs on to the table, 'then what message would you say can be read from these?'

Rebel closed her eyes to shut out the sight of photographs that bared her very soul. Photographs of Luiz laughing; scowling; cheerful; intent; Luiz basking in sunshine; swimming in the lagoon; Luiz cleaning the barrel of his rifle; Luiz standing in the midst of a crowd of young boys eager to acquire the skill he displayed in a strange new game called football! And dozens more pictures taken secretly, to be cherished and kept as a reminder, in the way a woman cherishes a locket containing the image of the man she loves.

Suddenly she knew that she could not bear to face Luiz's look of astonishment, Saffira's sneer of ridicule. Keeping her eyes averted, she jerked out of her seat and ran blindly towards the door. When her hand made contact with the knob she tugged it open and fled, leaving a memento behind her in the heavily silent room—an echo of a choked, heart-broken sob.

CHAPTER FIFTEEN

REBEL'S first instinct was to run to her bedroom, but halfway across the hall she changed her mind and veered towards the nearest exit, feeling the walls of the house closing in on her like a trap.

Outside, the night sky was ablaze with elements of electricity, a warning of imminent climax rendered all the more ominous because it was silent. Even the monkeys seemed too overawed to give voice as she ran from the house in the direction of the forest, hampered by slender, unaccommodating heels. If she had stopped to consider she would have had to acknowledge the foolishness of running for cover into a forest that at night time was more than usually inhospitable, whose spreading roots and patches of swampy ground were difficult enough to negotiate in daylight. But she was beyond reason, as panic-stricken and bewildered as a peacefully grazing doe who has suddenly been set upon by one of her own herd.

Mere yards inside the forest she was jerked to a halt, her skirt caught fast, spread colourful as a butterfly's wings across a bush of thorns. She tried to free herself, but the more she tugged the more the flimsy skirt billowed and became entangled within what seemed to her a thousand tiny fists determined to keep tight hold of their prisoner.

'It would seem, *senhorita*, that it is my lot in life to be always rescuing you from the consequences of your own folly!'

Her violent start caused a ripping sound loud enough to disguise the sob that tore from her throat at the sight of Luiz towering a few feet away, menacing as a hunter who has stalked and finally cornered his prey.

'Is there no limit to your foolishness?' he bit, striding savagely towards her. 'Haven't you stretched my endurance far enough by forcing me to chase after you into the interior; to rush you out of range of the headman's spears, then, on the homeward journey, to minister to the effects of a danger even a child would have had sense enough to avoid! Were you so unmoved by your previous exposure to freezing temperatures that you did not hesitate to risk spending yet another night in the forest, clad in a dress so insubstantial you might as well be wearing nothing at all?'

Shock jolted her rigid when, with a controlled violence far deadlier than any he had previously displayed, he ripped her out of the clutch of thorns, shrugged off his jacket, then whipped it around her shoulders.

'Do you feel warmer now?' he demanded so tightly a muscle kicked at the corner of his mouth. 'Warm enough to allow me to detain you just long enough to supply answers to some very important questions?'

She began a hunted protest. 'Yes, but ...'

'No ifs or buts, if you please,' he commanded grimly, 'just honest, straightforward answers.'

Suddenly Rebel began to tremble, not with cold because her blood was racing, her body hugged by the intimacy of a jacket still warm from the heat of his body. Misinterpreting the cause, Luiz breathed a curse and slipped his hands from her shoulders to enfold her in a featherlight embrace that expressed no more than a desire to comfort, a wish to ensure that she did not suffer the consequences of a chill.

She could not see his face, but his words sounded laboured when he accused over her downbent head, 'Why did you allow me to think that you intended to marry Paulo?'

'I didn't,' she choked, feeling suffocated by his close proximity, 'at least, not intentionally. When you broached the subject, I imagined that you were referring to my award.'

'And what excuse can you offer for your other deliberate deception?' he challenged dangerously. 'Why did you try so hard to project an image of worldliness, throwing out hints designed specifically to give an impression that you were as liberated as most girls reared in so-called progressive societies? You must have known that I dislike and disapprove of low moral standards, yet you persisted with your make-believe. *Why...?*

Suddenly her lacerated feelings rebelled against further humiliation, making it imperative that he should never know how his indifference to the love she felt for him had inspired her to act out a role totally opposed to her nature. Probably in the future, he and Saffira would speculate with amusement upon her contradictory behaviour, but at least she could deny them the satisfaction of knowing that she was every bit as naïve and unsophisticated as her father had intimated.

Proudly, she lifted her head to stare defiance into eyes grey as storm clouds, dense with the smoke of damped-down fires.

'What makes you so certain that I was play-acting, *senhor*?' She managed a light trill of laughter. 'I can excuse my father his outdated *mores*, but surely you are far too enlightened to expect women to be fragile, to blush at the slightest provocation, or to swoon if ever a man should push his amorous advances too far? I felt loath to rob my father of his illusions,' she mocked, 'but it did not occur to me that you also might be in danger of losing yours.'

'*You are doing it again!*' he gritted, sinking a claw-sharp grip into her waist. 'Implying that you are a she-cat who slinks through the jungles of the world in search of a mate. If that is really the case, then why was I so often left frustrated? I suspect that once again you are acting a lie,' he smouldered, 'which means that I am left with no alternative but to prove my theory right!'

Rebel struggled hard to avoid kisses that were a threat to her sanity, but he manacled her to his body with a steely arm, then grasped a rope of golden hair and held her head steady while he punished her without mercy for her trickery.

A lifetime later, when his kisses had drained her of all resistance, when her spirit had been tamed, leaving her a broken reed dependent upon his strength, she felt hands strong enough to wield a machete suddenly begin to tremble, saw uncertainty flash into eyes keen enough to enable him to sever the stalk of a flower with one shot.

'*Querida!*' he groaned, his voice tightly strained, '*meu bem anja*, never did I imagine love would be such torment, such an agony of doubt and uncertainty!'

Her senses reeled as if under the influence of the *epena* drug. Hesitantly she tried to speak, swallowed hard, then tried again.

'I don't understand—are you trying to make a fool of me, *senhor*?'

'No, *namorada*, I am not,' he denied with a mixture of pleading and anger, 'but could you really complain if I were, considering the way you have made me jump through hoops, manipulating my feelings in the manner of a trainer exercising power over a tamed circus beast! Since you erupted into my

life,' he continued to confound her, 'I have been
forced to cope with a whole new set of emotions.
You have rendered me confused, confounded, wildly
angry, tenderly protective, and for the past few days,'
his grip tightened as the admission was wrenched
from him, 'I have even had to fight a dreadful compulsion to murder Paulo!'

Tears blurred her vision as she stared at a face
that looked chipped from mahogany, doubting him
capable of such weakness, knowing she would have
found it much easier to believe that a mighty forest
tree could bend beneath the weight of a butterfly.

'*Say something, cara!*' begged the shirt-sleeved
devil trapped inside his own hell.

Her emotions felt lashed to the bone, making it as
much as she could do to tremble, 'How can I believe
you when you showed me as little respect as natives
show to wives who are offered to any overnight
visitor? Also,' the reminder brought her a pained
wince, 'you implied that you found me attractive
only because of the scarcity of women in the jungle.'

'When a man is taunted beyond endurance he will
resort to any form of defence,' he assured her quietly.
Then with a catch in his voice that lodged deep into
her heart, he abandoned all pride to apologise, 'I
bitterly regret causing you so much pain, *querida*,
and thank God that you are such a pathetically un-
convincing liar that I was never able to take advantage of your vulnerability, especially not during that
night of hell when you slept innocent as a child in
my arms—the night I realised that what I felt for

you was not merely desire but love, the sort of love a man can feel only for the woman he yearns to make his wife, the mother of his children.' Tensely he spelled out, 'I am asking you to marry me, *cara*; knowing how sensitive you are to the suffering of helpless animals, I'm certain you will not keep me waiting too long for an answer.'

'*Oh, my darling . . . !*' she cried out.

Incapable of further words, she melted against him and was snatched into the arms of Curupira— wild man of the Amazon that only love had managed to tame.

The Mills & Boon Rose is the Rose of Romance

Look for the Mills & Boon Rose next month

Doctor Nurse Romances

and November's
stories of romantic relationships behind the scenes
of modern medical life are:

DOCTORS IN CONFLICT
by Sonia Deane

It was love at first sight when Adam and Jessica met
in Amsterdam, and when he asked her to join his
practice in England it seemed like an invitation to
Paradise. But this Paradise, too, contained a serpent...

NURSE AT BARBAZON
(Summer at Barbazon)
by Kathryn Blair

Susan Day was asked to spend three months at a
Castelo in Portugal, as nurse-companion to a widowed
noblewoman. She was looking forward to her visit —
then she encountered the Castelo's imperious owner,
the Visconde Eduardo de Corte Ribeiro!

Masquerade
Historical Romances

Intrigue
excitement
romance

LADY IN THE LION'S DEN
by Elaine Reeve

When the proud Norman lady Adela de Lise was
kidnapped by the Saxon rebel calling himself Leowulf,
Lord of Erinwald, she refused to submit tamely. Then
she discovered that he intended to buy his own safety
by making her his wife . . .

UNWILLING BETROTHAL
by Christine James

Annabelle Sarne was doubly an heiress, but she had no
objection to becoming betrothed to her cousin Gaspard
— after all, she had loved him for years. But the
Revolution forced her to flee from France to England,
and there she encountered a man who had a prior
claim to her hand — and he refused to relinquish it!

Look out for these titles in your local paperback shop from
14th November 1980